John Codd

Voices of the Thames and other poems

John Codd

Voices of the Thames and other poems

ISBN/EAN: 9783337206437

Printed in Europe, USA, Canada, Australia, Japan

Cover: Foto ©Andreas Hilbeck / pixelio.de

More available books at **www.hansebooks.com**

VOICES OF THE THAMES

AND OTHER POEMS

BY

JOHN CODD A.R.I.B.A

Author of "A Legend of the Middle Ages" etc

PRINTED BY BUTLER & TANNER

FROME AND LONDON

1897

BUTLER & TANNER,
THE SELWOOD PRINTING WORKS,
FROME, AND LONDON.

TO MY DEAR WIFE

THE FRIEND AND COMPANION OF EARLY
AND OF LATER YEARS

I DEDICATE THESE VERSES

CONTENTS

VOICES OF THE THAMES

Looking Back

I LOVE thy wooded slopes, delightsome Thames,
    I love to stand upon thy grassy brink,
To watch thy waters ever flowing on,
    To gaze into thy liquid depths and think.

My spirit wanders down the glade which leads
    From past to present thro' the wilds of Time;
Unfettered fancy hovers o'er the past,
    And far away Life's bells so faintly chime.

A scene all dim, a tiny speck that fades
    Into infinity. An avenue whose lines

B

Converging, meet, and close with leafy bounds
  The pathway o'er which flickering lure-light shines

Till misty ether clouds the straining sight,
  What was commingles with what scarce had been ;
The picture blurred until the Restorer's hand
  Retouching paints anew the uncertain scene.

Those long gone ages, when a mightier growth
  Of fern and forest stemmed the sluggish way,
As thro' the spreading ooze it struggling, forced
  Thick mud-stained waters laden with decay.

  Through vast untrodden swamps,
  Dark Mammoth-haunted woods,
  Deep caverned depths
  Unlit by sun, or moon, or star,
      An endless twilight :
Where never scorching sunbeam gilds the gloom,
Nor dries sad Nature's tears ;
Where rainbow tints were powerless to unloose

The bands of Hope,

And with forgiveness conquer misery ;

When man, unconscious, slept in nothingness,

Nor yet had—waking—roused him to

  The dream of Life.

Myth

Those lowly mounds

Which break the softly undulating plain,

Once honoured graves of heroes

Who, in far-off days,

When Time was yet a child,

(We know not when,

So many cycles round and round have whirled)

Untaught, unlearned in Art's mysteries,

Those children of past ages strung

  The tinsel beads of Life.

Mysterious links which bind our flickering day

In fancy to the ever-fading past.

Green turf-clad barrows

Hide their crumbling bones,

Frail pigmy pyramids ;
And yet scarce less enduring than
Those statelier piles
Which after ages in another land
Upreared in massive stone
To shroud from ill
"The hollow-sounding chambers of the dead."

The past !
What myriad moons
Have circled round since, robed in flesh,
Those relics of an age unknown
Lived out their little span and slept again—
Slept undisturbed,
Their trinkets and their weapons close at hand
To serve their waking needs as in the past ;
Slept undisturbed, while base cupidity
Shrunk cowering 'neath the spectre eye of Fear,
While awe and reverence held
United counsel.

To-day the thirst for knowing reigns,

And awe and reverence are

As moonbeams in the noonday.

To-day the "Scientist" is king;

With prying finger he will point at what

      Was once a Pharaoh;

Toy with his household gods,

The riflings of his tomb,

Nor deem it sacrilege.

Time dulls the flash of Memory's mirror,

      Blunts her pencil point.

With the dead Time too is dead,

      And is not.

How lived our Father Man in those dim days?

      Did he, too, toil

For golden day-dreams as his sons do now,

And spend his life in the attempt to live?

Perchance a hunter,

With his skin-strung bow or flint-tipped spear,

Amidst the forest wilds or reed-bound swamps,

He tracked the huge colossus to its lair,

Half clothed in undyed skins;

His body decked with lines and pictures which

An infant art would joy to stencil,

In ochreous tints of yellow, black and red.

The far-off ancestor

Of many a cultured Dame of yesterday,

Whose beauty grew more beautiful when decked

With transient bloom.

Fair Nature diffident,

Distrustful of her charms,

Bowed down to Art.

He, too, perchance, from out the swollen stream

With line of wiry gut and hook of bone

      Drew scaly prey,

The huge progenitors of those,

The tiny perch or dace,

Whose 'minished numbers scantily reward

The angler's patient skill to-day.

A gruesome era, when the race of life

Was for the swift of foot,

And victory for the strong of arm,

And he who fainted died.

He lived, our Father Man, perchance he loved,

For man is man, and man was man,

And will be man throughout all time.

And she, the loved one,

Sang perchance for him her sweetest songs

And decked herself with borrowed graces, as 'tis now

And as it ever shall be till the end.

*   *   *   *   *

History

The Past is past. Fling open wide the door,

Time links the present to the never more.

He turns his glass, the hurrying sand runs on,

The spectres of an unknown age are gone.

Th' historic book lies open, and a scene
Of threatened conflict crowds the sloping green.
Two gathered hosts.   The flash of rival spears,
The shout, the tumult, fall on memory's ears;
A king, unwilling, signs his will away,
And dreams defiance on some happier day.
The victor nobles force the reluctant hand,
And Freedom's name is whispered thro' the land;
A cherished name in days of Saxon power,
When manhood claimed as man his manhood's dower;
A name scarce heard since, massed on Senlac's plain,
The power of England fought and fought in vain.
A Nation now re-frames its ancient creed
Of equal right on world-famed Runnymede.

Again Time hurries on, war's echoes thrill
Thro' copse and meadow, swamp and gorse-clad hill;
No sacred struggle now for ancient right,
No lightning flash out-bursting thro' the night
Of fierce oppression; not his country's weal,

For which the Patriot needs must draw the steel.

Ignoble strife, a land in blood to drown,

From brow to brow, to shift a tottering crown.

The old, old story. What does England gain

If other Tibnis die and Omris reign ? [1]

Echoes

Dim scenes awake, wild fancy roams afar,

    As idly flits the willow wren from tree to tree,

Or soaring upward thro' the wandering air,

    A tethered spirit, struggles to be free.

Old longings gather as the sunlight fills

    Each shadowy nook with soft reflected glow,

New vistas open in the azure depths

    Through which a maze of fleecy cloudlets flow.

The thrill of light, and life, and joy, and power,

    Th' immutable, unchangeable, the ceaseless song,

[1] 1 Kings xvi. 22.

The binding up into the sheaf of Life
Of all the pure, the true, the fair, the strong.

Onwards

    Swift moments pass away,
    Brief minutes may not stay,
    To-morrow is to-day.

    Short weeks on wings have flown,
    The months are not our own,
    Years pass and make no moan.

    Chill mists of morning rise,
    The mid-day glory flies,
    Day's vestals close their eyes.

    Life wakes with plaintive cry,
    Man waves his banner high,
    Spent hopes can only die.

Enchantment droops her veil,
Glad pleasure spreads her sail,
Smiles freeze and fall as hail.

Hushed is the voice of song,
The cry of pain is strong,
Time ever beats his gong.

Song, outbursting, overflowing,
Torrents gushing from the soul;
Now with transient sunshine glowing,
Now the crashing thunder roll.

Pain, the shrunk from, outward token
Of some lurking grief within;
Fairest promise rudely broken,
Gold transmuted into tin.

Toil, the burden, thankless labour,
Chain that rebel Will entwines,

Until it ascends its Tabor,
   And with love transfigured shines.

Crime, a festering foam scum, seething
   On sin's cauldron as it boils,
Pestilential vapours breathing,
   Folly's guerdon, passion's spoils.

Joys, the welcomed, meteors flashing
   O'er a dark tumultuous sky;
Silver-crested billows splashing,
   Flowers that wither, friends that die.

Dull remorse, a bitter longing
   For some pleasure passed away,
Surfeit on a dreary morrow
   Of the sweets of yesterday.

Life, the mystic, mazy tangle,
   Scented blossom, clustering thorn,

Sombre cloud with golden spangle,

Rose and nettle, tares and corn.

Growth

Adown its pebbly bed the gentle stream

In tiny ripples lisps its life away :

A prattling infant singing as it leaps

O'er bough and boulder on its heedless way.

From trickling fount to all-engulfing sea,

A suckling struggling in its mother's arms,

A truant speeding full of wanton glee,

A maiden decked in ever-growing charms.

A mighty force, resistless, uncontrolled,

A mine, a wealth, a flood of nerve and power,

A heritage to hoard, to squander, to enjoy,

One vast outpouring of glad Nature's dower.

Low, tender, trembling notes, half dirge, half song,
    Upon the rustling breeze are borne away,
While baby wavelets lap the pebbly brink
    In restless play.

A mighty voiceless stillness gathering floats
    Upon the pinions of the listening air ;
The stifled breath of silence mingling with
    A thrill of care.

Dawn

The stars look down from their bed of blue,
And light up the earth-stars of sparkling dew,
O'er the slumbering night fling a garment of snow,
And bathe it in light of long ages ago.
They glance into the waters so cold and fair,
And each one imprints its reflection there,
Till the concave above shuts its myriad eyes,
Growing dim in the light of the morning skies.

Awakening

Exultant Nature from the chill embrace of Night

Uprising, hides

Her radiant blushes 'neath a veil of mist,

Until the golden sun—

High father of her loveliness—

Dissolves the modest robe,

And to the eager eyes of worshippers entranced,

Who revel in her charms,

Unsought, unbidden, as with lightning flash,

Displays her changing graces.

E'en so the dusky moth or painted butterfly,

The child of darkness or of sunshine, each

Disdains the helplessness of babyhood,

The growth of youth,

And from its transient sleep,

At once imbued with all the instincts of maturity,

Bursts forth transformed

Into the fulness of a perfect life.

And now the sunlit air
Is filled with music,
And as with light its unseen atoms glow,
Wild melodies,
Now soft, now shrill,
Yet ever changing, mingling, blend
Into one gladsome song of joy;
Of ceaseless bustle, happy toil, unconscious life;
A life that teems with the exuberance
Of strength and motion, Nature's child,
Which lives, and knows not that it lives.

Daybreak

At early dawn the skylark shakes the hoar-frost from
    its wings,
And soaring thro' the blue expanse in exultation sings;
And as it upward, upward mounts yet softer falls the
    strain,
Then sudden ceases, with no song, it droops to earth
    again.

Luxuriant trees are decked with tiny crystals,

The soft caressing breeze allures

Alike the forest king and lowly shrub

To gentle laughter, and dissolves in showers

The glittering spangles.

And one, and all, in sweet unconscious rivalry—

Glad children of the sunshine—beauteous flowers,

Refreshed by silent sleep, and fed

With heavenly nectar,

Unfold their gorgeous petals.

Clamber now, o'er briery hedgerows,

Nestle 'neath

The tufted verdure,

Hide amidst

Impenetrable thickets,

Or bestrew the glowing meadows,

All ablaze,

With gold or purple.

Vest the lonely heath

In deep-dyed beauty.

Over stagnant pools outspread

A snowy carpet.

Burst in silvery blossoms from

The long green mermaid tresses as they sway

And surge and heave upon th' incessant stream.

New clothe the time-stained walls of cottage homes

With green and scarlet.

Mantle o'er broad level lawns,

With Nature's heraldry of azure, gules, and or,

In mingling blazonry.

Dear Spring, kind fairy godmother,

Whose magic wands,

Like Aaron's rod again are budding, blossoming,

Whose robes unfolding overspread

The earth with glory,

Till she whispers all unconscious of her ever-growing

    charms,

As the tender light of morning dances 'midst each

    opening spray,

Clothing with bewitching glamour Nature's bare and
 brawny arms.
O how lovely is the sunshine, O how beautiful is day.
Yes! Nature, thou art beautiful,
Th' enraptured spirit trembles 'neath thy power,
And humbly kneels in silent reverence.

Floating

The gentle current slowly drifts along,
 With here an eddy, there a flake of foam,
Its wavelets kiss the gay o'er-hanging flowers
 And softly whisper: "We are going home."

Home to that ocean where, forgotten, sleep
 The longings of so many mighty streams,
So many lives lived out, the grave of thought,
 The silent quenching of a nation's dreams.

The mingling ghosts of wandering echoes thrill
 The startled ear with hollow plaintive moan,

Delusive spirits, dead, yet lingering still,
  Weird phantoms of a life now all alone.

The flowing future ever hurrying on,
The ebbing past, too brief, too quickly gone;
Swift thoughts scarce live before they blend in one
      Unconscious aim.

New life awakes, develops, grows, displays,
Its gathering prowess, courts the wondering gaze
Of fear, love, adoration.—Passing days
      Leave but a name.

Motion

The humble-bee sweeps by on noisy wing,
  Caressing one by one the scented flowers,
He sucks the sweet, and revels in the fair,
  Exulting in the Summer's sunny hours.

The gaudy dragon-fly, its body twined
  Around as with a silken cord of green or blue,

Now here! now there! now poising motionless,
  Reflects light sparkles in each melting hue.

In jewelled robe the lustrous butterfly,
A radiant spangle, gently ripples by,
Its tints out-vieing e'en the wayside flower,
And like it living out its too brief hour.

The golden-hued Edusa gently floats,
  In tender dalliance o'er each flowery mead,
A gorgeous Io idly sits and suns
  Its plumage on the yellow-eyed hawkweed.

The dusky Atalanta, swift of wing,
  Sails by, or fastens on some favoured spray,
The tints of sunset deck its opening wings,
  The ruddy glow of Winter's snow-wreathed day.

And many another flitting, fluttering gem,
  Of deepest azure or of burnished gold,

Rejoicing in the glory of its day,
    For Beauty ever lives, and grows not old.

O Beauty! lovelier than the glancing ray which ope's
The shining gates of dawn,
For ever worshipped in thy mortal robe,
The treasured garment which alternately
        Allures, destroys,
The gods' own gift,
A glory to be worn and revelled in,
A fairy dream of love and trembling joy.

Instinct

The tiny fledgling of a year ago
Builds up its Summer home with all the practised care
Of skilled artificer;
Weaves for itself such fabrics as its race have twined
Throughout the ages;
Selects a kindred spot
In hedgerow, bank, or tree, or grassy nook;

Gathers up the withered bent, the feathers, moss, or
   wool,
As did primeval builders;
A style of architecture which knows naught
Of fickle fashion's changes.

    The noisy blackbird lines his nest
      With withered grass or hay;
    The sweet-voiced mavis rests content
      With finely tempered clay.

    The blue-winged tit on feathered bed,
      Her many nestlings rears;
    The rook re-forms with broken twigs
      Its home of bygone years.

    The robin chooses softest hair,
      For its connubial shrine;
    The linnet gathers moss and wool,
      Its Summer lodge to twine.

A few crossed sticks will scarce suffice,
　　The stock-dove's twins to hide ;
Blind dunnocks for the cuckoo's egg,
　　Unwittingly provide.

With rushes interlaced, the swan
　　Her shallow cradle weaves ;
The finches deck their villas with
　　Grey moss and withered leaves.

A hollow tree is shelter sought,
　　By jackdaw, starling, owl ;
The tiny wren, to nurse her brood,
　　Erects a feathered cowl.

And each and every with a wondrous beauty,
The purpose one, the method manifold ;
As varied as the pointed blades of grass
Which crowd the growing meadows in the spring ;

Or as the mingling strains

Of these, the swift-winged choristers,

Whose joyous carols fill the air with harmony.

Or as the changing thoughts

Which vibrate on the listening brain

Unbidden, numberless,

While Space and Time

The slaves of the material,

Fade, melt, and are not.

Or as the towering pinnacles which trace

The jagged cresting of some distant mountain range,

Arrayed in moonlight,

Glister and reflect

Each other's radiance.

Commingling

A fickle skiff untended floats

   Adown the placid stream the while,

As Fancy decks with witching lure

   The lover's vow, the maiden's smile.

And when the molten silver tide
   Basks in the mid-day's quivering glow,
Pale green o'erhanging osier beds,
   Their welcome shade reflect below.

A peaceful scene whose gentle charms
   The hurrying launch would fain invade,
As on with headlong haste it sweeps
   Thro' sunny heat, thro' cloud-lent shade.

The rush of life, an endless race
   Of mingling atoms surging by;
E'en pleasure's wings must flap apace,
   Or pleasure's self will droop and die.

The ceaseless rushing of a being which knows
   No more the holy restfulness of peace,
When turmoil, labour, care, are far away,
   And even Love's untutored longings cease.

Unbroken silence clinging all around,
　Or broken only by the ever-rippling song
Of tiny wavelets bursting into sheen,
　As o'er their pebbly bed they leap along.

A chaunt of restful life so sweetly sung,
　Low carols echoing back from shore to shore,
A story flashed in mazy beams of light,
　A trembling echo of the nevermore.

O! happy hours, absorbing all
　That hope, the Syren, dares portray;
An Eden, 'midst whose leafy bowers
　No tempter steals the soul away.

Where hawthorn blossoms drooping overhang
　The rushing stream, he plucks a snowy spray;
" 'Tis fitting that a flowery wreath so fair
　Should rest upon the brow of lovely May."

With artless coquetry the maiden twines
　Around her dainty turban's narrow brim
The scented bough, and then she softly smiles
　A wealth of happy memories to him.

But soon the fiery glancings of the sunny ray
　Have withered what but now was fresh and fair,
They idly fling the worn-out toy away,
　'Tis not the withered branch that love would share.

The Idol

　A lovely idol lured me once,
　　When days were young, and life was gay,
　High on a pinnacle it stood,
　　And seemed so very far away.

　It had a gentle dreamy face,
　　With wavy tresses long and fair,
　And just the shadow of a smile,
　　A tender smile half hiding there.

And all day long and every day,
    I knelt in spirit at the shrine,
Wherein my treasured idol stood,
    For I had learned to call it mine.

Embroidered robes of costly stuff,
    With gold and jewels spangled o'er,
A panoply of untold wealth,
    My idol all unconscious wore.

And as with timid, reverent awe,
    I humbly worshipped day by day,
My darling idol scarcely seemed
    To be so very far away.

And sometimes as I'd stand and gaze,
    A gentle murmur rustled by,
And I could almost dream I heard
    The echo of a trembling sigh.

Thus day by day more closely still
　My idol round my soul would twine,
As still with placid smile it stood
　A jewel in a jewelled shrine.

I longing gazed, and gazing mused,
　And musing slept, and sleeping dreamed ;
A wild, ecstatic sense of joy
　Above, around, within me beamed.

The idol I adoring dared
　To worship in its golden shrine,
Now clung around me, and I knew
　That it at last indeed was mine.

With eager hand and beating heart
　I tore its costly robe away,
Then with an anguished shriek I woke,
　My worshipped idol was but clay.

Opening Blossoms

Joyously, heedlessly, over the shallows creep
  Tiny skiffs laden with seekers of pleasure,
Toilers who labour and joy in their toiling,
  Singing in chorus the songs of to-day.

Slowly meandering, happy day-dreamers
  Listlessly paddle, or float idly by;
Moments are treasures but scantily treasured,
  Moments which wake neither laughter nor sigh.

Flow on ! upon thy bosom lightly borne
  The shallow punt which one fair maiden guides
With balanced motion, winning health's best dower,
  Breeze-painted blushes, and a world besides.

The sparkling wavelet's dancing sheen,
  The modest garb, th' unconscious mien,
Th' unstudied charms, the supple grace,
  And Nature brooks no second place.

The art of pleasing lives in seeming pleased,
   And Love, the gourmand, must on love be fed;
Each giving gladly—each receiving all,
   For self must die ere self can truly wed.

Drifting

   Drifting down 'neath the silent trees,
   Never a billow and never a breeze:
   Down! down! where the waters sink
   Fathoms deep by the sedgy brink.

   Creeping along where the beeches lave
   Drooping boughs in the limpid wave;
   O'er shingly shallows hurrying by,
   In ripples reflecting a quivering sky.

   Down the rough stony weir helplessly falling,
   Into the foaming pool noisily splashing;
   Deep in whose liquid depths, lost in the daylight,
      Tremble the silver stars.

Forsaken Channels

On its way surging,
    Lonely, deserted ;
Now by no iron-trod
    Towing path skirted.

Where the green osier beds
    Drink in its nectar,
Skirting the circling arc,
    Scorning its sector.

Haunt of no pleasure boat,
    No noisy steamer,
No tug or laden barge.
    Sought by the dreamer

Who in his lonely punt,
    Glides o'er its shingle,
Sport, leisure, death and life,
    Join, intermingle.

Life in its endless flow,
  Fiercely defiant ;
Now clear as sparkling wine,
  Calm, self-reliant.

Now but a turgid stream,
  Mist wrapped in sorrow,
Now bright with hopes of a
  Brighter to-morrow.

Now thro' the murky night
  Trouble encumbered :
Restless care pillowed where
  Love might have slumbered.

Now the night's starry lamps,
  Radiant with glory,
Shine in unceasing glow,
  Life's endless story.

Rest to the weary ones,
Peace to the sad,
Health to the sick at heart,
Sorrow made glad.

The Passing of Spring

Spring with unbound tresses coyly,
Streaming in the dazzling sheen,
Spring, the lovely blue-eyed fairy,
Wears her garb of dainty green.

Spring, whose joyous tears awaken
Sleeping beauties day by day;
Spring, whose smiles of gladness garnish,
Rocky steep and weary way.

Now with love-locks closely snooded,
Now with mien of queenly power;
All the pride of conscious beauty
Beaming in her golden dower.

Life's elixir, onwards, upwards,
    Fiercely thro' each fibre flows ;
Mingling 'neath the molten glory,
    Bloom the nightshade and the rose.

Scented sweets that grow and scatter,
    Lovely petals poison-steeped :
Budding, blooming, fading, falling,
    Fruit of harvests sown and reaped.

The Tempting Lure

There in a shady nook, hidden amongst the
O'erhanging branches which shadow the silent pool,
Warily, noiselessly, sits in his lazy punt,
Watching and waiting still, eagerly, anxiously,
Sits the keen angler, with patience exhaustless.
Is it the silly chub, darting in careless haste
Forth from his hidden lair, eager to gorge his full
On the deceitful lure, fatally ravening ?

Is it the belted perch, deep in the crystal depths,

Thirsting to feast upon dainties deceptive?

Is it the savage pike rushing with lightning speed

'Midst the young fishlings, which swifter still scatter?

    True as the bullet flies,

    Fiercely he grips the prize.

    Is it a *phantom*?

    The scaly roach, the shining dace,

      The barbel strong of will,

    Dull, sluggish bream and fiery carp

      The angler's basket fill.

    And king o'er all, the mighty trout,

      The prize of days of eager watch and wile,

    A trophy to be won and treasured up,

      If but perchance art can his ware beguile.

   The voice of Summer rings thro' copse and glade,

    The Summer gladness carols in the breeze,

Soft Summer whispers fill the scented air,
    Dense Summer verdure clothes the waving trees.

Sunshine and Tempest.

  On restless wing the swallow hurrying flits
    O'er copse and meadow, brake and dimpled dell :
  Now high in ether, now in voiceless speed
    Low circling skims the wavelets as they swell,
       And in the molten silver dips
       Its pinion tips.

A broad expanse of saffron grain, which sways
    In gentle billows 'neath the fluttering breeze ;
Afar, the busy reaper's whirring song—
    A ceaseless murmur as of myriad bees—
       Ripe ears the harvest toil forestall,
       Ungarnered fall.

With fury plumed the angry swan repels
    Intrusion in his realms, or proudly leads

His growing brood where low with craning necks
  They dive deep down amidst the bending weeds,
    And from their lengthening tresses steal
    A dainty meal.

With loitering step the lazy kine troop down
  To seek a tempting shoal which buried lies
Knee deep in silent waters ; there they stand
And whisk with tufted tail the teasing flies,
    As on the mysteries of fate
    They ruminate.

Expectant stillness creeps unseen around,
  A lurid glow lights up the murky air,
A gathering wind in rising tumult shrieks,
  Then sudden lulls in motionless despair
    As from the gathering sombre pall
    Huge rain-drops fall.

An instant rift divides the murky clouds,
  An instant flash illumes with dazzling glow
Each startled nook, and loudly roars aloft
  The furious din of battle.   Blinding flow
        Heaven's cataracts.   Is there on high
        No azure sky?

A growing brightness tips the melting mists,
  Soft raindrops fall in streaks of silver sheen,
Pale sunbeams mingle with the dust-strewn haze,
  And greener glows earth's robe of tender green;
        Commingling tints o'erarching glow,
        A perfect bow.

Securely moored the crowded house-boat lies
  'Midst furious blast, still heat, and pelting showers;
A canopy of drooping trees o'erhead,
  And decked with clustering galaxies of flowers.

The river-seeker's joy when skies are blue,

And snowy cloudlets veil the mid-day sun,

Or when the clustering stars exultant shout,

" We triumph now, the garish day is done."

The grimy tug, with short, spasmodic snort,

Against the sluggish current plods along ;

Deep-laden barges follow in its wake,

The river demon shrieks, his breath is strong.

Thirst

Fierce beat the sunbeams down on the withered turf,

Hot ! hot ! never a cloud ;

Earth to the children of fruitful Spring offers now

Only a shroud.

Glossy leaves fallen, struck by the glance of death,

Carpet the dusty plain ;

Nowhere to hide from the sultry air's scorching breath !

Come, gentle rain.

Trickling streams offer but scanty refreshment to
    Thy waning waters, O Thames!
Gravel shoals bask where they were not wont to do,
    Rain-drops were gems.

Weeds check the listless stream, deep eddies welling
    Up from the clear depths arise ;
Eddies whose sombre shades whirling reflect not the
    Azure-steeped skies.

Warblers are silent in thicket and tangled brake,
    Love notes could wake no refrain ;
Trembling leaves sigh as they sway on their slender
    stems,
    Thirsting for rain.

Flowers whose mingling tints gladdened their Mother
    Earth,
    Hierarchs of valley and glade,

Breathing no perfumed breath, hopeless their petals

    close,

    Wither and fade.

The Elixir

  The South wind blows softly, the warm breath of love;

    It ripples the stream, it caresses the flowers,

  And forth from the white clouds which mantle the

    blue

    Descend in bright pearl-drops the life-giving

    showers.

  The thirsting drink deep, and the parched-up no more

    Despondently drooping are ready to die ;

  The birds shake their plumes, and from thicket and

    brake

    Their glad notes of welcome are wafted on high.

  The sun which had glared on a withering world

    So stolid and sullen, with fierce torrid mien,

  Now lurks 'neath the cloudlets, now smilingly decks

    With spangles of silver the languishing scene.

As the crimson-tipped bud of the opening rose,

Or as vision outvieing the fulness of sight,

Or a beauty half hid, and affection that glows

Full of tenderness melting in shadow and light.

Existence all joy were a wearisome toil,

Sweet pleasure soon drowns in a sea of delight,

And day with its dower of glory and spoil

Fades silently into the stillness of night.

Drifting Clouds

The clouds of the daybreak are fleecy and fair,

The light of the daybreak is silvery;

My Love trips so gaily her garden around,

The birds and the flowers awake at the sound,

As she carols a sonnet of Spring.

The clouds of the morning are spangles of light,

The air of the morning is still;

My Love guides our skiff as we toil up the stream,
I bask in her sunshine and labour and dream
   That beyond is the haven of rest.

The clouds of the mid-day are dusky and grey,
   The light of the mid-day grows dim ;
My Love is my light amidst shadow and shower,
Her smile is my beacon, her heart is my bower,
   I dwell in my bower alone.

The clouds of the evening are purple and gold,
   And ruddy the fast-setting sun ;
In spirit my Love round my spirit entwines,
Clinging closer as day in its glory declines,
   And the twilight creeps silently on.

The clouds of the gloaming are misty and red,
   The light of the gloaming is fading ;

I silently sit in the shadow. Afar
Thro' the vista of years shines my youth's pilot star,
 As I wait for the gathering night.

Waning Fancies

Now the russet and gold of the Autumn are blending,
 Lit up by the flash of the kingfisher's wing ;
Aloft from the stubble of harvest up-soaring,
 The lark still re echoes its carols of Spring.

And now and again the wild outcry of struggle
 Is wafted along thro' the resonant air,
As athletes for laurels of victory striving
 In tumult commingle to do and to dare.

Resurgam

Where the quivering ripples flow stealthily down
And lingeringly cling to the skirts of her gown,
 Which the meadow-land trails in the deep.

Embroidered with tangle of rushes and reeds,
With gem-spangled petals, with light downy seeds.
   A rich harvest the soft zephyrs reap.

Breathe thou tenderly, Wind! o'er the slumbering life,
Weep, O Dew! joyous tears o'er the germ that is rife;
   With the vigour of ages gone by.
Enfold in thy mantle of darkness, O Night!
Emblazon, O Sun, with thy life-laden light
   The dry husks which Time's garners supply.

The dark waters surge up with a tremulous whirl,
And around in wild eddyings circle and curl,
   Ere they noisily hasten away.
Mystic thoughts treasured up in the storehouse below,
The dry grain, ages buried, now scattered to grow
   Into plentiful harvests to-day.

Ere the chill mists of winter spread over the scene,
While the hawthorn still mingles vermilion and green,
   Ere the voice of the nightingale's dumb,

There are flow'rets still blooming in dingle and dell,
Wild rivulets pent up, which bubble and well
  From the fountain of Summers to come.

The dim, fast-fading light of the lingering day
In a glory of golden haze hastens away,
  Broad-belted with purple between.
O ye light-suffused shadows! O promise of bliss!
The eager hand clutches, the longing lips kiss,
  For the grave of enchantment is green.

Down from their airy home flutter the withered leaves,
Hither and thither borne, slowly descending
      Till earth offers rest.
Softly the tender breeze whispers caressingly,
Whispers like sounding wings,
      What is is best.
Come! 'tis my mission to waft thee away;
Life, fruitful life, is the child of decay.

Life ! Not the same life.

No more shall the tender shoot

Bask in the sunbeam, or shrink from the hail;

Over the past, its growth, strength, and decadence,

Time, the relentless, withdraws not the veil.

Cold as a snow-cloud the white mist is swathing

　Dew-spangled meadows in mantle of sheen,

Slowly is fading the purple of sunset,

　Golden tints melt into palest of green.

Scarce opened blossoms fade away, and are not;

The fruit, when fully ripe, bestrews the ground;

Gay flowers, rejoicing in each gorgeous hue,

Their transient petals scatter and disclose

　The seed cells of the future.

Tall hedgerows glow with ruddy pearls, and 'midst the

　　naked trees

Pale clustered tufts of mistletoe sway in the gathering

　　breeze.

E

Assembling troops of birds prepare to wend their
    homeward way
To regions where. a warmer sun illumes a longer
    day.

The blackbird with startled cry hurries along,
    The plover on circling wing echoes its call,
The dove softly breathes a low, tremulous sigh,
    As slowly and gently huge snow feathers fall.

Retrospect

With a clamorous glee I ran down to the sea,
    When the summer sun was bright,
With a low rippling song, for the day-dream was
    long,
    And brief the unconscious night,
And I joyously bore to the far-off shore
    My burden of laughing light.

The gay flow'rets drink at my simpering brink,
    And look down thro' my depths below,

And I trill them a song as I hurry along,
  What is Life but a ceaseless flow,
And the golden light of the gathering night
  But the herald of morning's glow.

The bright trickling stream, like a silvery gleam,
  Dances down the steep mountain side ;
The pale, placid brook, a dazed wandering spook,
  Meandering far and wide ;
And the river that grows as it ripples and flows,
  In my gathering waters hide.

My dimples caught the sunny ray ;
  I kissed the drooping flowers ;
I bore their scattered seeds away,
For life was love, and love was play
  'Neath springtide's shine and showers.

But now the tiny streamlet flows a torrent fierce and
  wild,

The gentle brook that in the light of summer sunshine smiled,

Now rushes on in headlong haste, with muddy teincture
  stained;

The widening river seeks its goal, e'er strived for, yet
  ne'er gained;

Still-swelling streams on either hand, new-born of
  yesterday,

With eager, gushing hurry haste their tribute floods to
  pay.

I rush tumultuous thro' the plain, my placid surface now

Is clouded as I dash the foam from off my seething
  brow.

The supple osiers, terror struck, before my fury shrink,

I chafe against my crumbling banks, I top their grassy
  brink.

The music of my voice is lost in discords wild and harsh;

My teeming waters steal away to flood the rushy marsh;

No more is life a simple song, whose cadence dies
away

In strains which mingle with the past the longings
of to-day ;

But fierce and set, white-foam tipped waves, a purpose fixed and firm,

A gathering of life's atoms up into one endless term.

I hurry on with conscious might beneath a hope-
reft sky,   [they fly.

The pelting raindrops mingling with my torrents as

I rush between a gathering sea which spreads on
either hand ;

No prayer can check my onward course, no strength
my might withstand,

Till sullenly and wearily (one fate awaiteth all)

Into the everlasting deep, absorbed, engulfed I fall.

Gathering Care

Hoar spangles cling to the drooping shrubs—
The lilies are dead ;

A storm blast sweeps o'er the gathering stream—
  The swallows have fled.

No dragon-fly flits o'er the cowering meads,
  Or basks in the ruddy sun;
The wealth of the passing year is spent,
  Its pleasure days are done.

A daisy blossoming here and there,
  A buttercup hid in a shady nook;
Weary Nature has no other flowers to share,
  She has folded the leaves and has closed her book,
And the cold blast shrieks a discordant knell,
  'Thro' the husks of the lesser-clustered-bell.

The strength of the sunlight has melted away
  'Neath the grip of the gathering cold,
And the keen chilly breath of the frost-laden wind,
  For the tale of the summer is told.

Coming Night

In fan-like streams the sunbeams play,
A pall of light half veils the day ;
Unwearied birds in ceaseless strain
Their morning sonnets sing again,
Or flitting swift from bough to bough,
Forestall the springtide's tender vow ;
The listening air drinks in each sound,
And strews the lingering notes around.
Awake ! thou Queen of Ether, shine !
I love that tender light of thine,
A stream so gentle at its brink,
E'en lisping love may stoop to drink ;
Thy wild fantastic shadows fright
The silent loneliness of night,
And now the failing breath of day
In rainbow glories melts away ;
Dim haze its cold chill spreads around,
A veil whose fringe o'ertrails the ground,

While high amidst the liquid blue
White foam-flakes half obscure the view,
And soon the stars awake, and light
Their torches at thy shrine, O Night,
And glitter timidly till day
Shall chase their trembling light away.

  O mystery of day and night,
  O mystery of wrong and right,
  O mystery of love and strife,
  O mystery of death and life.

Sing, gentle strain, soft echoes thrill,
Awake thy potent power, O Will!
Thy halo o'er the future cast,
Smooth out the wrinkles of the past,
And thus the evening of to-day,
In joy and hope shall melt away;
The busy strain of life shall cease,
And twilight wear its robe of peace.

In hasty tumult feathery sprites commingling, fluttering
    fall,

And spread o'er Nature's fading life a dazzling snowy
    pall ;

With serpent hiss the quivering waves shrink 'neath a
    pelting hail,

Wild gusts of freezing vapour fill the keen relentless
    gale ;

Broad slabs of silvery whiteness gleam beneath a pallid
    moon,

And crashing, lurching, tumbling thrill the grim Night's
    dusky noon ;

The frost-fiend storms each sheltered nook, and grips
    the clustering reeds,

In tiny islands hurry down huge crags of tangled
    weeds ;

On surging floes the crusted snow in rugged heaps is
    piled,

Pale frozen ghosts of summer days gleam thro' the
    naked wild ;

Cold, grey-winged wanderers from the shores of distant ocean sweep

In circlings round the dreary waste of whiteness.
Slowly creep

The feeble tottering steps of age.   Dim is the lengthening sight,

While far-off childish laughter mocks the gathering
gloom of night.

The fury of the storm let loose, the evil of to-day;

Flow on, O river ! tempest torn, and bear thy load
away.

Waning Winter

The icy breath of Winter blows from o'er the Polar
seas,

Half-frozen drops of chilly rain drift on the hurrying breeze ;

Green leaflets cower beneath the blast, unopened
petals fall,

A cloudless gloom pervades the air, a sullen, dusky pall.

The sun, a spattered light-splash, gleams amidst th' uncertain haze,

Its glowing strength of heat and light now but a feeble
  blaze,—

The selfsame sun which yesterday in kingly glory
  shone,

And scattered wide a radiant glow from midst his golden
  throne ;

The selfsame sun —a sickly mist—a darkness dank and
  drear—

A dull miasma stealing thro' the cavern gates of fear.

Remorse, arrayed in sable garb, broods o'er the wreck
  of Time,

While Faith an ever-budding spring sees in a far-off
  clime :

Low, tender, summer voices melt in muttering sad and
  wild,

As tottering age re-echoes back the longings of the
  child.

Across the undulating meads pale flitting shadows steal,

Dim phantoms of a promised bliss scarce hide and
    scarce reveal ;

A listless silence fills the air, no strain of joy uptends,

Suspense sits cowed in leafless bower, a chilly mist
    descends ;

The lingering ghosts of pleasures spent, fantastic outlines
    trace,

And for their shadowy footsteps find no certain resting-
    place.

Fair Hope, in weary longings, hides amidst the thicken-
    ing shade,

The dove's low mournful cooings fill the air-spent
    breathless glade ;

In sullen gloom the swollen stream pursues its ceaseless
    way,

No gladsome ripples, laughing sheen, no song, no
    sportive play ;

The weary whirl of busy life, the wheels' incessant round,

Joy's scanty waters poured on dry and unreceptive
    ground ;

No blinding hail, no thunder crash, no tempest black
    as night,
But just a dull and listless gloom, no shadow and
    no light.

Optimism

    Hope lights her fairie lamp, and deems
    She sees amidst th' impenetrable darkness
        Sure promise of a coming dawn ;
    She spreads her wings intangible,
    And self-sustained, unaided soars
        Thro' space illimitable.
    Deems every noisy chime a marriage bell;
    Sees in the lightning flash a transient glimpse
        Of light ineffable ;
    Hears in the thunder peal but the refrain
        Of angel music,
    And when the furious tempest howls and shrieks,
    Erects huge barricades across the path of Fear,
    And waits unmoved the coming calm.

Hope is its own remembrancer, it writes

In flickering sunbeams stories of the future;

It imprints its sterling stamp on every base alloy,

And unabashed repeats again the hackneyed tale

    Which flutters on the uncertain wind.

Unstable Hope! whose syren smile too oft has lured

The victim to his doom, and fed the vampire mouths

    Of dull despair,

Her brow is ever garlanded with flowers,

And to the victor's laurel wreath she ever points

  exultingly,

    But grasps it not;

She raises high the shout ot triumph

    Ere the fight begins;

A very Berserker, she scorns impenetrable armour,

And rushes to the fray as though invulnerable;

She scorns defeat, to death impervious.

Hope grasps the shadowless impalpable,

And space and time to her alike are phantoms,

Deceivers, or deceived, or both.

Parables

    The robin hops on my window-sill,
        And chirps for his daily dole ;
    The sparrows squabble and scold and fight
    From early dawn till the close of night,
    And whether in play or whether in spite,
        They over and over roll.

    Two rocky banks bound the riven way,
        A torrent foams between ;
    Dull sheep on the sun-browned hillside graze,
    And look at me still with their stolid gaze,
    As they did in those early far-off days
        When the pastures of life were green.

    The bells ring out from the ivied tower
        Their stories of joy or woe,
    The moon looks down on the spreading plain,
    The nightingales warble the old sweet strain,

And after the sunshine that follows the rain,

The purple-robed clouds hurry back again

    And shadow the amber glow.

A blue tit climbs on the leafless twig,

    The morning sky is grey;

The silvery brightness of April rays,

The midsummer sun with its scorching blaze,

The golden glory of autumn days

    Have melted in turn away.

The mountain slopes are with snow-wraiths white,

    The rainbow tints them still,

The heart with its longings unfed grows cold,

The fancy has little of wealth to unfold,

The pictures of life are no longer of gold,

But hopes, wishes, fears in one purpose are rolled,

    The purpose of steadfast Will.

Rook-heralds encircling the elm-tree tops

    Proclaim the o'erspreading dawn;

Tho' gathering earth-clouds prevent the light
And mists, the pale children of dusky night,
The spirit of life in its ceaseless flight
Speeds on to the endless morn.

Fair Promises

Again the tufted blossom-buds their opening tints
display,
The sallow's lengthening tresses droop in streams
of feathery spray ;
The banners of the tardy spring are one by one
unfurled,
As loving sunshine melts the chains which bound
a frozen world ;
Huge snow-wraiths float in middle air, with golden
glory crowned,
And earth and air re-echo life in life's unceasing
sound ;
Marshmallows fringe the lazy stream with clustered
orbs of gold,

F

The leafless fruit-trees vie in haste their treasures to
　　unfold ;

Mauve cuckoo flowers stud the grass, the cuckoo's
　　voice is clear,

And Hope, the king of coming days, shakes high his
　　glittering spear.

Reverie

Silently, dreamily, with eyes bent on the ground,

Unthinkingly, yet full of thought,

I wander on, with no set purpose filled,

As when a lazy boat unguided drifts

Adown the stream unheedingly,

Now whirling slowly in an eddy, now

A moment tangled in some sedgy bank,

And turning hither, thither, as a Will unseen impels.

Then hurried on in headlong race,

On some swift current borne resistless.

Vague, wandering thoughts, which flit

As martins o'er the silver-burnished stream

In ceaseless circlings,

And instant change from sunlight into shade,

From doubt to gladness.

                 Now lingering o'er

The softened outlines of a present past

In all its tenderness of melting hues,

Now wafted effortless thro' th' illimitable

While Will and Mind in soft oblivion sleep,

And Fancy, unrestrained,

Luxuriant revels in

The misty indistinct which guards

The threshold of the Future.

The Song of the Leaf

        In the early springtide,

           Shaking off the snow,

         Big with future greatness,

           I began to grow.

Fairy visions of Life seemed to gladden my view
As I basked in the sunshine and drank in the dew.

Clad in virgin beauty,
　　Flowers spread all around,
With disdain I scorned them,
　　Grovellers on the ground ;
For I deemed that—a dweller in visionless air—
I should burst into blossoms more precious, more rare.

Swelling with the longings
　　Of a life untried,
Glad I rend the trammels
　　Which my glories hide.
'Midst a forest of leaves I perceive with dismay
That I too am a leaf quite as common as they.

Waiting all impatient
　　Thro' the lingering night,
In the early daybreak
　　Reaching to the light,

To imbibe in its essence the life from on high,
Crushed by crowds of keen rivals as eager as I.

    Whispering to the breezes
        As they loiter on,
    Sighing as the moonlight
        Tells of daydreams gone ;
Whilst the thrush floods with harmony forest and glade,
It is mine but to scatter one spangle of shade.

    Burnt with noontide kisses,
        Trembling 'neath the blast,
    Bruised by pelting hail-drops,
        Holding, clinging fast
For dear life to my home on the storm-riven bough,
'Tis existence, not light, that is all to me now.

    Wet with clinging hoar frost,
        Bright delusive sheen,
    Russet tints replace my
        Summer garb of green.

On the wings of the rushing wind wafted on high,
'Midst my fallen companions I nestle to die.

Refrain

The echoes of passing days bear along
The lingering notes of forgotten song,
The life of the loved and lost,
The life of the borne away,
The cold clinging breath of the shadow of death,
The idol with feet of clay.

The Glory Departing

From the horizon a mellow glow, spreading, expand-
ing, creeps silently upwards ;
Night's purple canopy, lifting and paling, melts, and
is lost in the soft haze of daybreak ;
Light, the Awakener, drinks up the dewdrops around
morning's eyelashes clinging ;

Icy the ground, iron-fettered, resounds with the mingling
  clamour of hurrying horse-hoofs;
Forest trees, shivering, scatter around them the chilly
  night's glistering spangles.
Day in its glowing life thro' the dim ether thrills, melting in softest blue;
Clustering cloud-wreaths float o'er the azure, embroidered with edging of silver,
'Neath which the sunny rays hide from the soul-chilling
  breath of the north wind.
Fleecy mists, light-laden, hover and cling round the
  skirts of the desolate marshland;
Fiercely the turgid stream sweeps on its headlong way,
  fatefully swollen;
Down by the frozen brook, stately and lonely, the heron
  stands watchfully resting;
Soaring aloft thro' the keen air, the song of the skylark
  exultant is pealing;
Shadows of sombre night melting are lost in a radiance
  reflecting the glory ineffable.

Life

There is a mystery above, around, within,
A power which permeates and fills
Infinity.
Th' unfathomed mystery of ceaseless being;
Which is, and passes, which for evermore
Is reproduced, and perishes,
For ever waning and for ever new.
The flower that seeds, and withers, and decays;
The forest tree, which year by year renews
The wild luxuriance of youth.
The tiny atoms which, innumerable, crowd
Into one fleeting day their all of consciousness.
The myriad denizens of land, and sea, and air,
For ever preying on the weaker, and themselves
In turn the prey of other—stronger, swifter, mightier;—
These, and a myriad more
Of untold organisms,
Each in its own degree imbued

With what in all its infinite variety

Of growth, of conscious and unconsciousness,

Bears but one title—*Life*—

All in their tiny, weakly helplessness

Enter upon their constant journey; and,

Be this their span a passing hour,

Or be it lengthening ages,

All, like the sun, attain their zenith,

And, like it, together wane, decline, and are not.

In *these* volition, instinct, purpose, will;

In *those* but growth.

And one and all

Are lost in seeming nothingness, and yield

No hostage to the future.

And e'en their ruler, Man,

With all his bootless strivings for

The unattainable,

His ever-restless clutchings at

Illusive phantasies,

His wild, unstable dreams of good and evil,

Ends but in silence,

Even as the beasts that are, and perish.

Is it peace?

Forgetfulness of pain, and care, and ill,

A happy longing that for ever grows,

And evermore

With newly-opening flowers of bliss,

Is ever satisfied;

Which sips at will the crystal cup of joy,

A cup which fails not.

Or is it but a waiting nothingness?

Not e'en a fading dream, to link

The yesterday with what may be hereafter?

And that hereafter!

Who shall unfold the riddle of eternity?

Unseen to vulture's eye, outlying far

The mystic bounds of wisdom's searching ken,

The spirit's pathway to its essence, or

The way which leads the finite atom to the Infinite.

It but remains to gather up and hoard

The grains of dust which cling
Around the trailing skirts of the Illimitable.

Flow on, O purling stream !   Flow on,
And bear me gently on thy placid tide,
While yet I dream the flitting dreams of time,
And struggle, helpless, in the web of destiny,
Whose tender gossamers of liquid light,
Intangible, elude, yet ever bind.

The Awakening

Wild spirit voices in mingling lay
Welcome the birth of the coming day.
Hurricane shattered,
Tempest torn
Scattered cloud-flakes
Greet the morn,
Ruby tinted, hurrying by,
Weeping in a sunlit sky.

Streaks of purple,

Dense and cold,

Bar the sunset's

Field of gold.

Transient glory,

Fading light,

Melting into

Gathering night.

The Woof

The shout of the laughing river,

    The rush of the pent-up breeze,

The voice of unbroken silence,

    The whisper of clustering trees,

The flash of the mellow sunbeam,

    The splash of the pattering rain,

Each tells in its turn a story

    Of joy, of regret, of pain.

The song of the Summer sunshine,

    The wail of cold wintry days,

The fulness of Autumn's bounty,
   The Springtide's unceasing lays.

The hopes of the cloudless morning,
   The noontide's meridian light,
The evening's lengthening shadows,
   The chill of the deepening night.

The track of the quivering moonbeams,
   The glance of the planet's ray,
The depths of the purple stillness
   Which heralds the coming day.

The pride of unlooked-for triumphs,
   The torture of hopeless pain,
The storm of unfettered passion,
   A lullaby's low refrain.

The whirl of the rushing tempest,
   The moan of the dying day,

The sob of the ebbing wavelets,
　The dew of the scattered spray.

The thrill of a new-found feeling,
　A longing but half expressed,
A dream of unconscious beauty,
　The moan of a soul unblest.

A flash of the sunlit ether,
　A flood of unceasing rain,
A veil of fast-falling snowflakes,
　A dream never dreamt again.

The roll of a mighty organ,
　The mirth of a bridal throng,
Wild strains as in trembling cadence
　They melt into silent song.

Thro' all in their changing changes,
　Its life one unending day,

The breath of the foaming river
  Ebbs ever and ever away.

Thro' all in its hurrying tumult,
  Its cravings which never cease,
It flows on its way for ever
  To the haven of promised Peace.

New Life

With ceaseless whirl the stream of Life pursues its
  restless way,
And once again the flowers of Spring bedeck the
  lengthening day ;
E'er varying tints of tenderest green the opening
  leaves unfold,
And rival in their lusty life the Autumn's garb of gold.
The leafless blackthorn first assays to put its garment on ;
Then plum, pear, cherry, each in turn, their snowy
  raiment don ;

With timid blush the apple blossom bursts its ruddy
    sheath,
The gorse with spangled wealth of gold bedecks the
    lonesome heath,
The chestnuts' petaled pyramids their waxen sweets
    display,
And all day long the robin sings its welcome to the
    May;
The gentle primrose nestles in its bed of dewy
    green,
The widely spreading meadows wear their robe of
    golden sheen;
The lily decks the shady wood with petals frail as
    fair,
And purple-streaked anemones the welcome shelter
    share;
Fair Spring displays her mingled charms, her shadows
    and her showers,
And with the growing strength of youth adorns her
    transient bowers.

Flow on, O River! on thine endless way,

    Thro' field and meadow, copse and tangled dell,

Thro' scenes of deeds on history's page engraved,

    Thro' scenes where history's strain again shall swell

        In mingling song.

Flow on! Flow on thro' all the changing years,

    And bear new treasures to the far-off sea;

Rejoice, exult, the glories of to-day

    Are but the dawnings of the power to be

        When Life is strong.

Circling Ages

    Round and round in endless cycle

      Summer sunshine, Winter cold,

    Spring and Autumn, germ, fruition,

      Time the hoary grows not old.

Billows of the tideless ocean
  Splashing, foaming evermore,
Melting into lisping wavelets
  On the calm eternal shore.

Years that bristle o'er with passion,
  Love and sorrow, toil and rest,
Eager, ardent, worship of the
  Sunbeams on the mountain's crest.

Days that know no waning twilight,
  Ages that are ever young,
Mantle of the Great Eternal
  Over past and future flung.

Years speed on and leave no ripple
  On eternity's vast sea,
Myriad ages past and passing
  Limit not what is to be.

Flow on, O River! on thine endless way,

    Proclaim thy mission with unwearied voice ;

The gloomy night of nameless fear is past,

    The watched-for morn awakes. Exult! rejoice!

THE SNOWDROP

I saw a pale bud springing
   From the womb of its mother, Earth,
Clear sparkling dewdrops around it clinging,
   Glad morning's tears of mirth.

Thro' the frozen turf upbursting
   It shakes off its mantle of snow,
For life's eager visions of pleasure thirsting,
   And Spring's exultant glow.

I watched each leaf unfolding
   'Neath the smile of the fostering sun,
Skilled Nature's hand with chaste beauty moulding
   The leafy web she spun.

The gentle showers descending
　　With new vigour endue each vein,
Till the snowy blossoms, their green sheath rending,
　　Drink in the welcome rain.

I beheld her in beauty blooming
　　With a modest, retiring grace,
As the shadows of clouds in the distance looming,
　　Stole over her gentle face.

The storm blast round her sweeping,
　　Close she clings to her mossy bed ;
And silently cold rain drops weeping,
　　Mourn over the scattered dead.

The dusky cloud vail fleeting,
　　Her clear gaze greets the azure sky,
Outpourings of mellow light lovingly meeting
　　Her pensive, glistering eye.

The Springtide's keen frosts blighting
   O'ermantle the tender flower;
No more shall she bloom in the sunbeams delighting,
   Or greet the refreshing shower.

Death's chill grasp round her twining,
   Her fair petals has tinged with decay,
And calmly her head on the greensward reclining,
   She pines her life away.

AN EVENING REVERIE

'Tis evening, and the round hill tops
  Of Malvern pierce th' unclouded sky;
Their verdant summits and the blue
  Ether appear in rivalry.

The narrow path winds far above
  The varied surface of the plain,
And hazy distance shrouds the view
  As distance veils the unruffled main.

The straggling village lies below,
  Its storm-worn abbey seems to be
A tiny model of itself
  In an unknown infinity.

Beyond, cloud shadows lengthening creep
  Across the distant wide expanse,
While favoured spots more brightly glow,
  Lit up by Day's expiring glance.

Behind, sheep idly stand and graze
  Upon the gorse-clad, steep hill sides;
And on the breeze of evening borne,
  The gathering darkness softly glides.

The daylight glories pale and fade
  Like hopes ungathered, nursed in vain,
Or kiss from lips of dear one loved,
  Or distant musick's echoing strain.

And now the first of those bright gems
  Which nightly spangle o'er the skies,
With ever-growing lustre lights
  The lamp of gathering memories.

Fair visions silently steal by,
  Of love light, clear as brightening star,
In streams of glory floating round,
  A beacon answering from afar.

Soft blows the evening's fading breeze,
  Low whispering round th' untending ear ;
O little man ! a dust speck borne
  On Time's swift pinions year by year.

But yet man's restless strivings bear
  The impress of unconquered Will,
The boastings of a soul which dares
  To bid the rebel floods be still.

And now the golden sunlight fades,
  Grey twilight hardly intervenes ;
Already eve's blue misty vail
  Has fallen o'er the distant scenes.

Now myriad tiny spangles deck
　Th' empurpled canopy above,
Their quivering rays but dimly light
　The footprints of the God of Love.

Grim darkness wheels its hosts around,
　Proclaiming silently, " 'Tis night";
The breeze on which they seemed to float
　Lies buried in the grave of light.

Chill deathlike silence reigns alone,
　It thrills the soul with startled awe,
O'ercrowds the sense with forms of fear,
　Pervades each hurried breath we draw.

But hark ! a tender, soothing strain,
　The wandering rill skips o'er its bed,
And softly to the silent ear
　Sings requiem for the daylight dead.

Melodious strains, so sweet, so full,
   Low echoes trembling on the ear,
Half sad, half full of gathering hope,
   Comminglings of a smile and tear.

Its notes dispel the fearsome awe,
   And soothe th' oppressive sense of care ;
Low whispers full of tenderest trust,
   Of treasured thoughts we read and share.

Now rising moonbeams quivering flood
   The dusky caverned gloom of night,
The distant Severn winding glows
   A silver trail of molten light.

The placid radiance spreads and drives
   Each shadowy form of fear away ;
Life's dark, uncertain storm-drifts melt,
   And night reflects the light of day.

A WAYSIDE BALLAD

PART I

*A slight Sketch of the Life and Thought of a Country
Village in the Earlier Years of the Century.*

WHILST one with Earth's uncultured flowers
   A priceless garland weaves,
Another opens Nature's book
   And idly turns the leaves.

Whilst one on Fancy's wings will soar
   In wild exultant strain,
Another like the swan to rise
   From earth attempts in vain,

And many fritter life away
　In an unceasing round
Of business, pleasure, toil or play,
　Time's bell gives but one sound.

A little village maiden lived
　In days now long since flown ;
Around her life a story clings,
　A story scarce her own.

The village, quite a rural one,
　A laggard in the race,
Its scattered homes unconscious of
　The luxury of space

Yet rich in charms but little known
　To toilers cooped in towns,
Its scented fields, its grassy lanes
　And undulating downs.

Wide spreading woods, where pheasants roost,
  Broad cultivated leas,
And here and there a scattered farm
  Half hid amongst the trees.

The Hall, a square built modern house,
  With ugliness pourtrayed
Upon its many-windowed front
  Its stuccoed balustrade,

Surrounded by a wealth of lawns
  And gardens gay with flowers,
With winding pathways, terraced shrubs,
  Quaint nooks and shady bowers.

Below it groups a gabled pile,
  Outliving time and change,
The manor house of years gone by
  But now the manor grange ;

Its long, low rooms, its massive walls,
 And mullioned windows quite
Absurd appear in days when art
 Must yield to space and light.

The ancient smithy by the green,
 The village stocks hard by,
Used only when some saucy rogue
 The luxury would try.

Beyond, the one old-fashioned Inn—
 The Squire would brook no more—
His crest, a beehive, as a sign
 Hangs creaking o'er the door.

The church, half hid 'midst dusky yews,
 With ancient roofs and screen,
And crumbling carvings which reveal
 What it must once have been.

And still o'er many a grassy mound
    Its lengthening shadows fall,
The loved, and mourned, the lone, unwept,
    The shadow [1] rests on all.

The priest, a tall ascetic man,
    Of slow and stooping gait,
With Naboth's accusation bans,[2]
    Each foe of Church and State.

A pathway from the village green
    To Jessie's dwelling led,
Close by the pound, across the stile,
    A walnut tree o'erhead,

Sweet woodbine decks the rustic porch,
    Around it roses twine ;
Fair Peris by their fragrant breath,
    Allured might stay and dine.

[1] Symbol of God's Providence.
[2] " Naboth did blaspheme God and the King " (1 Kings xxi.
13).

A wild old-fashioned garden rich
   In bright-hued perfumed flowers,
Where countless bees hold revel in
   The Summer's sunny hours.

Here little Jessie's early years
   Passed unobserved away,
The father made her quite a pet
   And never said her " Nay."

The mother, too, with cords of love
   And maxims neat and kind,
Would constant strive life's straying twigs
   Round duty's stem to bind.

Thus Jessie grew as daisies grow,
   A lively, loving sprite ;
Her mother called her noisy romp,
   And she, no doubt, was right.

H

She'd tear her frock, and scratch her hands,
    As country children will,
But then for this she made amends,
    For she was never ill.

With dimpled, round, and rosy cheeks,
    A pleasant sight to see,
And pale grey eyes which sparkling shone
    In merry happy glee.

A lilac pinafore and hood
    On "work-a-days" she wore,
Short skirts, and warm grey worsted hose,
    And boots laced up before.

But on a Sunday she'd appear
    In hat of russet brown,
With marguerites and corn flowers wreathed
    Around its low flat crown.

And morn and afternoon alike
    To church she'd always go,
And sit as children used to sit
    On benches in a row.

The school, a long low room, o'er which
    The broad-leaved ivy climbs,
Stands sheltered from the Western gales
    Beneath a row of limes.

The mistress, short, and sharp, and thin,
    With curls of chestnut dye,
Sits prim, and levity repels,
    For naught escapes her eye.

Here Jessie learned to knit and spell,
    To sew, and write, and read,
And "do addition"—that was all
    Girls then were thought to need.

Once every year in Summer time
   The Squire was wont to make
A luscious feast to all the school
   Of firmity and cake.

At times like these his children, too,
   Would join the party there,
And in the noisy rustic games
   Delight to have a share.

So Jessie grew, and Time sped on
   With steady, careless stride,
Until a first deep shadow fell,
   Her mother drooped and died.

And now, bereft of all beside,
   Her father needs her care
To scatter sunshine o'er his home,
   His lonely lot to share.

So Jessie went no more to school,
  Tho' she was only ten;
She kept her father's house at home,
  There were no " standards " then.

Five happy, busy, growing years
  On hurrying wings have flown;
A deeper shadow crossed her path,
  And Jessie was alone.

O'erwhelmed with grief and heedless of
  Aught that could now befall,
With passive acquiescence she
  Was sheltered at the Hall.

And there she learned unnumbered things
  Which she had thought she knew,
For all the maids were very glad
  To give her work to do.

And quickly Jessie found a friend
　　Amongst the maidens there,
With whom she spent the careless hours
　　Which duty left to spare.

Together, 'midst the fields and woods,
　　On Sunday evenings they
Would often wander and enjoy
　　A sylvan holiday.

And sometimes James, the youthful Squire,
　　Would meet them in their walk;
They could not but be flattered by
　　His merry, lively "talk." [1]

Now this, in Mrs. Grundy's eyes,
　　With utter flagrance shone;
But Jane and Jessie never thought
　　To put her glasses on.

[1] Conversation, a provincialism, now nearly obsolete.

And James himself was quite a boy,
  Brimful of saucy fun ;
And loving, more than all beside,
  His beagles and his gun.

His lady mother quickly heard,
  With undisguised dismay,
How Jane and Jessie and her son
  Met every " Sabbath " day.

'Twas spiteful Rumour told the tale,
  And she, as usual, knew
A great deal more about them all
  Than was exactly true.

So Jane, the elder of the two,
  At once was sent away;
But Jessie begged, with timid tears,
  To be allowed to stay.

To Litwick James was hurried off—
The school in fashion then
As much or more than it is now
Amongst the upper Ten.

And Jessie, grown quite stout and strong,
Was to the laundry sent;
It might not be her fancy, but
She strove to feel content.

And time flew by, and day by day
The daily work was done—
A life that told its passing years
But by the circling sun.

But Sunday was a gala day
And, in her best arrayed,
Would Jessie go to church and then
Came sunshine 'midst the shade.

For Jane an elder brother had,
  And he would sometimes call
To see his sister when she lived
  With Jessie at the Hall.

And even after Jane had "left"
  He'd often come to say
That Jane was well, and sent her love,
  And then he'd talk and stay.

Now Thomas was a joiner, he
  Was quick and clever too ;
The Squire employed his master for
  What work he had to do.

So Thomas to the Hall was sent
  Whenever things went wrong;
He did not mind the tedious walk,
  Nor deem it lone or long.

And tho' the laundry might not need
　Any especial care,
Yet Thomas, when his work was done,
　Was sure to linger there.

For Jane a place was quickly found
　At the adjoining town,
And, as the doctor's parlour maid,
　On Jessie she looked down.

And Jane increased in beauty as
　The laggard months passed by ;
She wore a fashionable dress
　And bonnet on the sly.

For in those days the maidens were
　Expected to be neat,
And not to ape the costume of
　Their "betters" [1] in the street.

[1] A very common provincialism at that time.

And James, just grown to man's estate
    (He was at Oxford now),
Aspired to stroke his college eight—
    At present he was bow.

But when term ending brought him home
    He'd find, almost each day,
Important business at the town
    Which would not brook delay.

On farrier or on gunsmith he
    Would be compelled to call,
And, anxious for his health, he sought
    The doctor most of all.

The time passed on more slowly now
    For Time will often stay
His headlong course, and linger o'er
    An uneventful day.

And Jessie, nearly twenty-two,
  Had grown sedate and staid;
Her wages too were raised, for she
  Was second laundry maid.

And she and Thomas seemed to grow
  Into each other's ways,
And in their evening walks they'd scheme
  Their plans for future days.

Tom's master at one time had had
  A comfortable trade,
And he had taken care of all
  The money he had made.

But as for "going with the times,"
  Of that he never dreamt,
And that "new-fangled contract work"
  He viewed with much contempt.[1]

---

[1] A general feeling at that time amongst tradesmen of the old school.

So more and more each passing year
    His business went astray,
And rivals gathered what he seemed
    Resolved to fling away.

And now, when Thomas felt that soon
    He'd have no work to do,
The Squire one morning sent for him
    And said, "I've plans for you.

"I want a handy, useful man
    To live on the estate ;
I much respect your master, but
    He's getting out of date."

"And here's a house just empty, and
    Your earliest work shall be
To build yourself a joiner's shop,
    Built as it ought to be."

"Amongst the farmers all around
   You'll find employment too;
In fact, I've very little doubt
   There's work enough for two."

"And should you think of married life
   You possibly may find"—
He said this with a genial smile—
   "A damsel to your mind."

So Jessie found a happy home,
   And Tom a gentle wife,
As peacefully she floated down
   The placid stream of life.

For Thomas had by sheer hard work
   An honest penny turned,
And careful Jessie had not quite
   Expended all she'd earned.

Old Time had smiled on Jessie, too,
    And smoothed her tangled hair,
And sprinkled freckles o'er her cheeks,
    For health was blooming there.

And Jessie made a prudent wife,
    Her every thought was bent
On spreading o'er their modest home
    A halo of content.

    *   *   *   *   *

And now a letter came from Jane,
    The first since long ago
She'd left the doctor, and was gone
    Where, no one seemed to know.

She wrote of care, of failing health,
    Her husband dead, her boy
Just twelve months old, her longing for
    Her home, its restful joy.

She wanted not for this world's goods,
　　She'd plenty and to spare;
But for her child the mother's heart
　　Was full of anxious care.

She was alone, her weary life
　　Drew very near the end,
And she would like once more to see
　　Her brother and her friend.

To Jane a hearty welcome came,
　　And for her boy a home,
And life's dull waves were bright again
　　With flakes of sunlit foam.

But all in vain, the waning life
　　Passed with the waning year,
And Nature decked the wintry grave
　　With many a frozen tear.

And when the early Spring was gay
　　With resurrection life,
A marble tomb was reared, inscribed,
　　"To Jane, my loving wife."

And on that smoothly polished stone
　　So cold, and white, and bare,
Were graven words of burning love,
　　Half sorrow, half despair.[1]

With many voices "Wonder" spoke,
　　"Surprise" was present, too,
And "Idle Gossip," ever quick
　　To say a word or two.

But Jessie, while her tears fell fast
　　Upon the grassy mound,
Clasped in her arms the orphan child,
　　And love its guerdon found.

[1] There is such a tomb and inscription in a Church not very many miles from London.

For very soon the little one
  Around their hearts had twined
His thread of life, and they'd no will
  The tangle to unwind.

Now passing seasons hurry on,
  And Tom has prosperous grown;
The tall, fair boy is all his pride,
  As tho' he were his own.

And work brought wealth, and wealth of wealth
  Would multiply the store,
For he who has, the scripture says,
  Shall, having, have the more. [1]

PART II.

And can it be that thirty years
  Have passed as one away?
And what was youthful vigour then
  Is middle life to-day?

[1] S. Matt. xxv. 28, 29.

That passing years old age have led
  Unto its silent home?
That raven locks are now as white
  As sea-waves' crests of foam?

The Squire has passed away, and James,
  His son, the Squire is now;
A man of business, somewhat keen,
  Frank eyes and open brow.

And James, I should have said "Sir James,"
  This is his title, he
Has three times for his county stood,
  And now he is M.P.

Such claims a grateful country has
  At all times well repaid;
And he, the meed of triumph won,
  A Baronet was made.

My lady, first in gentle care
　For every rustic ill,
With quite a troop of daughters, who
　Well emulate her skill.

Louise, a beauty, laden with
　The budding cares of life ;
For she'd a year ago become
　A neighbouring rector's wife.

Then two whose ages differ but
　A twelvemonth and a day,
And dubbed by witty friends " the twins,"
　So much alike are they.

And Dora next, a fair-haired maid,
　Who, eighteen years ago,
Was but a tiny helpless mite
　That scarce had learned to crow.

But now her father's darling, who
    Is ever at his side,
Companion of his evening stroll
    Or of his morning ride.

So full of wondering love for all
    The beauties round her spread,—
The golden meads, the waving trees,
    The changing skies o'erhead.

Amidst the fields and glades she loves
    To spend life's early hours,
With no companions save her friends—
    The trees, the birds, the flowers.

To wander thro' the thick pine woods,
    Whose branches arching o'er
Break up the sunny rays, and strow
    Their fragments on the floor.

Here startled rabbit hurries on
  Across the narrow "ride,"
And stock-doves wake the echoes of
  The quiet eventide.

Nor unexplored the quarry depths,
  With bush and briar o'ergrown,
Where ages past to build the church
  Was dug the hard grey stone.

'Twas here the choicest flowers would bloom,
  Tall ferns and grasses wild,
She'd pass the spot with creeping awe
  When yet a timid child.

A tragedy long years ago
  Had made it haunted ground;
And even now weird shadows seemed
  To tremble at each sound.

Fair Dora dreamt a fearsome dream;
   Wild terror and dismay
Clung round her, till an angel dashed
   The shapeless fear away.

A horror, what, she knew not, 'twas
   So indistinct and dim,
And yet so mighty that it seemed
   Help could but come from him.

Now Tom and Jessie both had lived
   Their unobtrusive day,
And comforts gathered round them as
   Life's summer passed away.

And Thomas had, so common then,
   Though rarely met with now,
His pigs and sheep, his geese and fowls,
   His pony, cart, and cow.

The babe had grown into the boy,
　The boy into the man ;
At school and college, work and play,
　He struggled to the van.

A scholarship he'd early gained
　Inspired to something more,
And then success upon success
　To Oxford ope'd the door.

At thirty-one his earnest work
　Was not unknown to fame,
And honour's fitful halo seemed
　To hover round his name.

The quiet, dreary, dull old town
　With life is thrilling now,
And simulates the smile of youth
　Upon its furrowed brow.

The village, too, no longer sleeps
 The sleep of other days ;
A railway floods with bustling haste
 Its rustic winding ways.

The ancient church has put away
 Each passing age's whim ;
Its "thorough restoration" leaves
 It new, and neat, and trim.

Its ceilings, galleries, green baize pews
 Alike have given way
To open benches, timber roofs—
 The fashion of to-day.

The Hall, in its old lavish style,
 No longer ope's its doors ;
And neighbouring tradesmen much resent
 Its dealings with the stores.

For times are not what times have been,
And rents have fallen low;
The farmers scarce a profit reap
On anything they sow.

Sir James has much ado to make
His lessened means provide
For growing needs; impatiently
He waits the turning tide.

A hearty welcome at the Hall
The young Professor found;
His novel, socialistic views
Were sown on fertile ground.

For time had hurried by since he
Had sought his early home,
And in another name he'd sought
To rear Ambition's dome.

And who could recognise the babe
  Who, thirty years before,
Unconsciously a suppliant came
  To Tom's and Jessie's door,

As now, o'er wearied with his work,
  He seeks a quiet rest?
The childless joiner's vacant rooms
  Oft welcomed such a guest.

And he, too, in the fields and woods
  Would often idly stray,
To gather lichens, mosses, ferns—
  His hobbies of to-day.

Fair Dora's heart reached out to one
  Who seemed so far above,
And yet, whose accents thrilled with all
  The tenderness of love.

To teach and learn, when each delights
   In what is learnt and taught,
Unconsciously the listener thinks
   The sympathetic thought.

And Dora fancied she could trace,
   In outline faint and dim,
That mighty angel of her dream,
   So like, yet unlike him.

The happy days and weeks flew by,
   And ere the parting came,
He offered her his heart, his all,
   His prospects, and—his name.

His name—a name that sounded strange,
   And yet not all unknown,
'Twas graven thirty years before
   Upon that cold white stone.

And then—some other pen than mine
  The story must unfold;
For tears are but a fickle stream,
  And love is never old.

A broken heart, the one farewell,
  So tender and so true
And then—the wild and dreary waste,
  And life begun anew.

While idle songs are gaily sung,
  One saddened soft refrain,
The cooing of the widowed dove,
  The ne'er to be again.

The shadow of a simple cross
  Falls on a grassy mound,
Another young and ardent heart
  Its silent rest has found.

With Tom and Jessie now life's tide
    Flows sluggishly along ;
Its laughing ripple hushed, it sings
    A hollow, plaintive song.

Nor is Sir James at all the man
    He was a year ago,
He stoops a little in his gait,
    His hair is flecked with snow.

The car of Time unceasingly
    Pursues its noiseless way ;
The strong may love, the fair may die,
    The striver win the day.

The fly lives out its little life,
    The student can no more,
His dearest aspirations float,
    Mere wreckage to the shore.

In far-off lands where England's sons,
  A growing empire raise,
The once Professor sadly lights
  The lamp of other days.

To be, to do, to live, to toil,
  As in the long ago ;
To sow the seeds of future weal,
  Let others watch them grow.

Success or loss, above, below,
  But finite words which tell
What transient shadows flitting by
  Have dreamed of ill or well.

And tho' the passing breeze's breath,
  The chaff may whirl on high,
Yet many a grain of wheat is left
  To die and fructify.

The bat which aimless flutters round,
   Half dazzled by the light,
Amidst the deepening twilight breaks
   The shadowy gloom of night.

The glories of the rising sun
   Illume a well-run race,
But daylight's early hours are torn
   From midnight's chill embrace.

The craving heart so cold and dead,
   Alike to praise or blame,
Alone in silence kneels before
   The memory of a name.

Life, waning life, can offer but
   A valueless renown;
The shadows of the past have reft
   The idol of its crown.

"BETWIXT TWO WORLDS LIFE
HOVERS LIKE A STAR 'TWIXT
NIGHT AND MORN"

BYRON

SUNSHINE and pleasure,

    Sorrow and cloud,

Gaily decked cradle,

    Flower strown shroud ;

And 'twixt the one and

    Other outspread,

Lives of the living,

    Deeds of the dead.

[1] Star of the morning,

    Paling away,

[1] Job xxxviii. 7.

K

At thine uprising,
　　Ruler of day ;
Star of the evening,
　　Shining more bright,
Thro' thy blue panoply, ·
　　[1] Beautiful night.

[2] Sing, star of morning,
　　Thro' endless days,
Anthems of glory,
　　Worship and praise.
Sing, star of beauty,
　　Sing, star of light,
Sing, as thy radiance
　　Gladdens the night.

[3] Not through thine own being,
　　Not by thy power,
Trembling intensity,

[1] Southey.　　　[2] Job xxxviii. 7.　　　[8] Zech. iv. 6.

Betwixt Two Worlds

Hour by hour.
Thro' years and ages,
  Stedfast alone,
Like and yet unlike
  Life on its throne.

Life as it might be,
  Light from above,
Shedding around it an
  Infinite love.
O, happy life lived,
  Life yet to be,
Light that may shine thro'
  Eternity.

MAY

I DREAMED a dream of lovely May,
Of sunshine all the livelong day,
Of quivering heat, of shady bowers,
Of meadows spangled o'er with flowers;
The lark on quivering wing on high
Its carols thrilling through the sky;
The sylvan stream with ripples bright
Reflecting back the sunny light;
The hawthorn's robe of scented snow,
The coy laburnum's golden glow;
The gentle breeze whose timid sigh
In soft caresses rustled by;
The throstle's joyous song, which made
Sweet music in each leafy glade;
The cuckoo, whose incessant voice

Sang gaily, "It is spring, rejoice,"
And then to my delighted eyes
The fair Hyale was my prize.

I shivering woke, my noisy sneeze
Scarce heard amidst the rushing breeze,
And, oh! the sharp rheumatic pain,
I wish to—never sneeze again.
The surging trees, swept by the blast,
Their scarce unfolded verdure cast;
The frozen and unfrozen rain
Beats loud against each window pane,
And o'er their moisture-reeking beds,
Pale flowerets hang their drooping heads;
Cold dusky storm-clouds hurrying fly
Tumultuous o'er the murky sky;
A gleam of sunshine, and again
Falls thick and fast the pent-up rain,
The torn wind howls; I turn away,
And feel that it indeed is May.

SUMMER, 1892

THE passing summer melts away,
To-morrow glides into to-day,
Its waves have broken into spray,
　　And drifted over.

I've quaffed dame Nature's richest wine,
The breeze which blows across the brine,
And felt its essence gladden mine,
　　But now 'tis over.

I visited in turn each spot
Where Earth has drawn her loveliest lot,
Where irksome business cares are not;
　　Alas! 'tis over.

The sunny South allured me first,

When Springtide with deceitful burst

Of sunshine hopes of brightness nursed,

    Too quickly over.

I wandered by the Western shore,

Where wild Atlantic billows roar

And spend themselves, and are no more,

    Their fury over.

I turned my steps to hilly Wales,

And there amidst her crags and vales

I drank ozone : but what avails,

    For it is over.

I sought the North where heather grows,

Its mountains capped with Summer snows,

Where time and money quickly goes,

    Till all is over.

O Dying Summer : We whose lays
Denounced thy cold and rainy days,
Look back on thee with longing gaze
Now thou art over.

A DAY'S EXCURSION TO LONDON

FOR a long Summer's day we were wending our way
    to Town on that morning early;
Those not up too late had their hair combed straight,
    the rest had to wear it "curly."
Some who claimed to be wise had not closed their
    eyes for fear that they might not be waking,
And one—said a friend—ere her slumbers would end,
    had required a merciless shaking.
The grim shadows of night seemed to circle us quite,
    an impalpable indigo awning,
And the clock striking one, that it's time to be gone,
    sounds a hollow and lingering warning;
All our party close packed, for we space rather lacked,
    we drive on with steady persistence,

And on looking around, 'twas the first time we found
 that we'd heard of each other's existence.
Two old farmers whose size was almost a surprise,
 a slim damsel with cheeks pale and sallow;
In a corner tight squeezed a young couple quite pleased
 to lay down life's plough land to fallow;
Then a good-humoured dame, rosy cheeks, rather lame,
 with a bird cage and parcels in plenty,
And a lovely young thing, quite a bee on the wing,
 whose age was—she told us—just twenty;
A young man and his wife, who are drifting thro' life,
 she his duck, he, her darling old gaby,
With no moment to spare as with boisterous care,
 they hush the unhushable baby.
Rural hamlet and town, meadow, coppice, and down,
 each in turn as we pass are receding,
Thro' a tunnel we rush, up a steep incline push, and
 anon o'er the level are speeding:
That weird spectre of night, the white owl in its flight,
 its defiance indignantly screeches,

And we start at the cry of a peacock close by, at roost
in some wide-spreading beeches.

We scarce try to think out a thought or to link our
ideas, we all are so sleepy,

And the night's chilly breath like the cold dew of death
clings around us, damp, chilly, and creepy.

With an effort some strive to keep small talk alive,
but the most are dull, heavy, and weary,

And remarkably slow comes the "Yes," "Eh," or "No,"
the reward of attempts to be cheery :

Each fair lady her smile hides away for a while, as
she sits with drooped eyelashes dozing,

And in turn one by one or in half unison, all our
mouths we are opening and closing.

The old joke and the tale are of little avail, to wake
up our slumbering party,

E'en the jocular man, let him try all he can, soon
subsides with his laugh loud and hearty.

All our wan faces seemed as tho' each one had deemed
that to wash was too great an exertion,

Or 'twas rather a seeming that we were still dreaming
　　of trains and our joyous excursion.

No one cared to complain tho' it spattered with rain,
　　for we had not the spirit to grumble,

But we took what befell, be our lot ill or well, we
　　were all so subdued, meek, and humble.

In a comatose state thus we slumber and wait, till the
　　sun finds its time for arising,

And then we too awake, off our drowsiness shake
　　in a way that is really surprising ;

Just a yawn of surprise, then a rubbing of eyes, soon
　　the ladies their toilets are making,

And they quickly display in their own charming way,
　　an appearance bewitchingly taking.

Then a craving within prompts us all to begin, what
　　at least is a pleasant diversion,

For to eat and to drink most excursionists think, is *the*
　　charm of a charming excursion.

Quite a small husk of chaff now awakens a laugh,
　　and we all have a repartee handy,

Almost every remark as it falls strikes a spark, as we
 quizzical compliments bandy ;

As the train speeds along one commences a song,
 with a long-drawn mellifluous chorus,

But our voices fall flat as we realise that, there's a
 toil of sight-seeing before us.

We grow silent once more, a long journey's a bore,
 that at least seemed the general feeling,

And hot, hasty, and short, passed the quip and retort,
 "on their sleeve" each one's true self revealing.

As the sun rises higher, some feel they require fresh
 air, the compartment's so stuffy,

One complains of the cold, others angrily fold around
 them their wraps soft and fluffy.

All at once the train slows and we rather suppose
 we shall stop at the town we are nearing,

And the ladies with glee, talk of hot cups of tea ;
 but, alas ! there's no station appearing,—

Just a small country town, narrow streets up and down,
 busy men to their day's work are wending :

With its station they say a good half mile away,
  Noisy chaff with their grain of wheat blending.
Now we're getting up speed very quickly indeed, and
  past station by station we hurry,
For our train, somewhat late, has got into a state of
  bustle, excitement, and flurry.
The two stout farmers say they shall finish the day
  at the " Palace," that garden of pleasure,
They have tossed for a dinner, and he who's the winner,
  exults in his luck without measure.
Streets and houses appear, and it's perfectly clear
  that we've almost completed our journey.
The funny man sighs and with woe-begone eyes, says
  he's come up to see his attorney ;
The old dame did intend to arrange with a friend
  to come to the station to meet her,
But she's lost the address and is bound to confess
  she's afraid that her memory 'll cheat her.
Every one has a plan the brief hours to span with a
  bridge of unceasing enjoyment,

All assured of a feast for a day at the least,
 undisturbed by the ties of employment.

Now we trundle along midst a newly-built throng of
 trim villas, pert streets, anon stopping ;

Then we move on once more, and soon stop as before,
 like a lady whose mind's bent on shopping,

And at length we arrive as the clock's striking five,
 and with spirits as light as a feather,

We all promise to meet when we've finished our treat,
 and to make our way homeward together.

WAITING

CHILLY breathes the breath of Even,
  Faintly shines the moon,
Chilly blows the breath of Even;
  He will be with me soon.

Lengthening shadows on the greensward
  Slowly fade away,
Lengthening shadows dim the greensward;
  Why does my own one stay?

Rosy hues of sunset linger,
  Timid stars appear,
Rosy tints of sunset linger;
  My Love, I feel he's near.

Twilight grows more dark and sombre,
    Night dews round me fall,
Twilight looms more dark and sombre ;
    My Love comes not at all.

Shadows glide across the moonbeams,
    Thrills my heart with fear,
Shadows mingle with the moonbeams ;
    My Love, my Love is here.

SONGS OF LIFE

THE CRAVING

"The eye is not satisfied with seeing, nor the ear filled with hearing."—*Eccles.* i. 8.

O why not ever thus? The longing cry
For bliss just tasted as it flashes by ;
Th' insatiate thirst, which drinks, and drinks in vain,
Its craving unallayed, it thirsts again.

O why not ever thus? Th' enchanting thrill
Which brain and soul and spirit seems to fill,
As heap on heap are piled the golden toys,
And trembling fingers clutch at fancied joys.

146

O why not ever thus? The sheltered glade
Reflecting life in sunshine and in shade ;
The tender murmuring of the clustered leaves,
The blue above; around the golden sheaves.

O why not ever thus? Th' o'ershadowing night,
The silver moonbeam's gentle quivering light,
The o'erflowing heart, sweet words, whose tender tone
The loved one hears, and feels them all her own.

O why not ever thus? The present seems
More blest than fancy in her wildest dreams
Had dared to picture. Heart and heart made one,
And, for a moment, Paradise re-won.

O why not ever thus? Th' exultant song
Of him who triumphs 'midst the motley throng
Of toilers fainting, struggling to attain
The glory he has won? Toil all in vain.

O why not ever thus? The weary one,
His strivings o'er; the day's work nobly done,
Its voices hush, its anxious cravings cease,
And rest is joy, and bliss unbroken peace.

O why not ever thus? Scarce conscious being,
Past, Present, Future, one vast boundless scene,
A subtle essence linking heart and brain,
A dream that—waking—sleeps and dreams again.

O why not ever thus? The spirit fraught
With wildest dreams of wild, unfettered thought,
To stem, unaided, Life's untrammelled stream,
Regenerate man the thesis of his theme.

O why not ever thus? Th' o'erwearied brain
Exultant teems with glowing thoughts again,
Quaffs breezy nectar as it ripples by,
And feels again Life's essence fructify.

O why not ever thus? No care or toil,
No weary striving for precarious spoil;
To eat, to sleep, the flowers untended grow,
But touch the sterile rock and waters flow.

O why not ever thus? The mystic goal
Absorbing all the longings of the soul;
Commingling life, in dual union twined.
The soft, low breathings of a summer wind!

O why not ever thus? The soul's one dream—
Ambition, Knowledge, Love; the cherished scheme,
Whate'er it be, the sought, the craved, the prized,
Life would be Life, were it but realized.

"O why not ever thus?" The saddened voice
Of longings mingling with the cry, " Rejoice !"
The ceaseless echoings of a far-off song;
Glad joy-bells muffled by the wail, " How long ? "

O why not ever thus? Again, again,
The transient bliss, the all-absorbing strain,
Alluring phantom! Bride, whose bridal dress
Is but a shroud—to have and not possess.

O why not ever thus? The cry of Life
In all its eager toil, its ceaseless strife;
A lingering echo from a far-off shore,
A fickle glamour luring evermore.

THE LAMENT

"The strong shall be as tow."—*Isa.* i. 31.

O WILDERNESS of aching hearts !
   O wail of passing day !
Unuttered longings twining round
   The life that wanes away.

O memories of th' unfinished toil,
   Of scattered pearls unstrung ;
Electric meteors quenched in night ;
   High pæans left unsung.

Of work which lacks the master-touch,
   The mystic charms which thrill
Thro' all, when ready heart and hand
   Obey the guiding Will.

O cheering word ! O strong right hand !
   O voice of days gone by !
Fond memories of a living past ;
   A pent-up stream run dry.

Across the unseen spirit-land
   Life's breezes gently blow ;
A passing breath alone divides
   "To long for" from "To know."

O weight of sadness gathering o'er
   The ne'er-forgotten past,
As sorrow-laden tempest clouds
   Their deepening shadows cast.

To watch the weary tide of life
   Ebb silently away,
The vision of to-morrow but
   A picture of to-day.

The nerve-racked brain whose listening ear
  Shrinks, tortured, from each sound,
The merry chirping of the bird,
  The baying of the hound.

Dim quivering flame whose flicker lights
  The outreaching mind alone,
A bell untuned, its low sad toll
  A hollow, nerveless tone.

Awake! awake! O sleeping life;
  Frail weakness, be thou strong;
Wild dirge! thy saddened wailings cease;
  Raise, Hope, thy joyous song.

Ye pictures fair of summer days,
  Why will ye rise again?
Pale, soulless phantoms mingling with
  The cold, unceasing rain.

The rainbow, born of Nature's tears,
  And sunshine's transient glow,
A glory melting as those tears
  Of gladness cease to flow.

O stifled cry of riven hearts,
  Sad voices of the night,
When shall the forest gloom roll back?
  The morning stream with light?

Dead joy-notes pealing from the lost,
  Faint echoes from afar;
The fickle, intermittent ray
  Of some dim, distant star.

The withered flower, the fallen leaf,
  The twilight's lingering gleam,
The hollow moaning of the wind,
  The phantom of a dream.

THE AWAKENING

"Cast thy bread upon the waters, and thou shalt find it after
many days."—*Eccles.* ii. 1.

WHERE the acorn fell on its peaty bed,

But the toy of the blustering gale,

There the forest king holds his leafy court,

·And exults in the tempest's wail.

Mighty chaos reigned o'er a world submerged

'Neath the waves of despairing Night;

At the voice of the Mighty transformed it glows

With a flood of pervading light.

Where the giant elk in the days long past

Roamed at will o'er the tangled wild

Mighty cities teem with a growing wealth,
  And the mart is the desert's child.

O'er the scattered atoms of mouldering dust,
  And of bones that are very dry,
There is moving again the renewing breath
  Of the Spirit which cannot die.

Midst the mingling tissues of good and ill,
  Of regret, of delight, of care,
Which the weary seekers have gathered up,
  Which they worship, and grudge to share;

In the time-chained garb of a living death,
  In the growth that precedes decay,
As a flickering lamp in a cavern's depths
  Shines the light which we call "to-day."

But the morrow dawns, and the nerveless hand
  Feels the breath of the mountain air,

And the weak is strong with unfailing strength,
  For the promise of life is there.

While the rivulet joyously bounds and leaps
  On its way to its far-off goal,
But a tangle of light in its mountain home,
  Into ocean vast billows roll.

The bewildered brain in vain strivings lost,
  Now exults in a fadeless glow;
For the shadowy dreamland of Time is past
  And "to be" is to love and know.

A LENGTHENING VISTA

O GIVE me back my early youth,
  The hours which flew unheeded by,
The fulness of a virgin Hope,
  The light of Faith's unclouded eye.

O happy, merry, gladsome days,
  So free from toil, and care, and thought,
With rippling laughter brimming o'er,
  The joyousness of joy unsought.

The vision of a fairy scene;
  The world a wealth of joy for me,
A butterfly's unclouded life;
  Weird moonbeams shimmering on the sea.

So near, and yet so long ago;
   A dream that can be dreamt no more,
An anchor buried in the sand,
   A phantom ship which finds no shore.

O give me back the home I loved!
   When life was strong, and brave, and young;
When o'er the future's promised bliss
   No requiem had as yet been sung.

The modest dwelling, on whose hearth
   Life's mouldering memories grow not cold,
But, fanned by love's undying breath,
   Glow brighter as the days grow old.

The narrow-bordered gravel path,
   With daffodils and lilies gay,
And tufts of many an old-world flower
   Whose names have almost passed away.

Green waving meads and scattered woods,
　Where many a wild bird—rarer now—
Had yearly built its springtide bower,
　'Midst tangled brake, on leafy bough.

O forge again those broken links
　Which bound me to the unfading past,
Again around those cherished scenes
　The glamour of affection cast.

Fast friends, whose lives were part of mine,
　Like shadowy dreams have passed away;
The fair, the strong, in youth, in age,
　With raven locks, with tresses grey.

And you, dear loved ones, most of all,
　Around whom brightest memories twine,
Within whose hearts I dwelt alone,
　Whose *all* of love and life was mine.

The old grey church, beneath whose shade
The hopes of generations sleep,
The joyous clang of marriage bells,
The turf-clad grave where loved ones weep.

Huge spreading elms, amongst whose heights
The sweet-voiced mavis loved to sing,
Their cavern depths, whence nightly swept
The harsh-voiced owl on labouring wing.

Low grassy slopes, round tree-clad knolls,
Vast cornfield crests of ruddy gold,
Green shady lanes, wild gardens where
Dear Nature's loveliest flowers unfold.

The fruitful autumn's teeming wealth,
The summer evening's golden glow,
The budding loveliness of spring,
The winter's veil of dazzling snow.

M

Still through its level marshy plain
　　The mighty river hurries by,
'Midst changing scenes alone unchanged,
　　It sings its own soft lullaby.

The soaring lark in gladness pours
　　Its wild exuberance of song ;
While, tempest-tost, life's banners wave
　　O'er buried hopes a countless throng.

Amidst the mist-enshrouded maze,
　　Where gloom and sunshine mingling reign,
Scarce can the practised eye discern
　　'Twixt growing wheat and worthless grain.

O opening life, so bright and fair,
　　Adorned with all to charm and woo ;
O crumbling life, a hoary wreck !
　　The sought-for false, the shrunk-from true.

Ye glories of the moonlit sky,

  Star-spangled canopy of night,

What mean ye to the wearied eye

  Which scarce reflects one gleam of light?

O loved and passed! a living dream

  Too sweet, too dear to melt away,

Time-hoarded relics treasured up,

  Soft echoings of a far-off day.

ENROBED in majesty, the Saviour reigns;
His glorious presence fills the heavenly plains
With golden radiance.[1]   An unnumbered [2] band
Of holy Seraphim adoring stand
Before His throne, and in exultant song
Proclaim His praise.[3]   A myriad spirits throng
The heavenly courts, rejoicing in His sway,
And at His feet their happy homage pay;
Themselves His ministers,[4] who e'er fulfil
With joy the dictates of His loving will,
While all their radiant panoply is bright,
But with the beams of His pervading light ; [5]

[1] Rev. xxi. 23.   [2] Rev. v. 11.   [3] Rev. v. 12-14.   [4] Rev. xxii.
9, and Heb. i. 14.   [5] Rev. xxi. 23.

And e'en the strains of harmony divine,

Which fill the lustrous air when angels twine

Their wreaths of praise, imperfect, but express

Some faint reflection of His holiness.[1]

How then shall fallen man, sin's vanquished slave,[2]

Whose life is but a journey to the grave,

The chief who rules, the monarch of a day,

The humbler serf who tills his kindred clay,[3]

How shall he kneel before the eternal throne,

Where angels' worship mingles with his own?

How shall his trembling lips assay to plead

His Saviour's merits for his constant need?

How shall he pray?   How can he hope to raise

On earth the echoes of angelic praise?

At first the banner of the frozen world

Amidst chaotic darkness was unfurled.[4]

As changing eras slowly sped away

---

[1] Job xv. 15.   [2] Rom. vi. 16-23.   [3] Rom. ii. 11.   [4] Gen. l. 2.

Their countless ages, but a passing day
In the Creator's sight, earth grew more fair,
Till man, in God's own image, worshipped there;
His work was finished, the All-Wise surveyed,
And sealed approval on the world He made;
Six heavenly days sufficed Him to fulfil
Creation's work by His all-potent Will;[1]
The seventh day He set apart and blessed,
That it should be a day of holy rest,[2]
For man ordained,[3] beneath this earthly sun
Type of his endless rest when life is done.

In after ages Adam's offspring reared
Their household altars to the God they feared;
And, taught by Him, a sinless victim bled,[4]
An offering He accepted in the stead
Of all who in the sacrifice descried
The Saviour's one atonement typified.

[1] 2 S. Pet. iii. 5.   [2] Gen. ii. 2-3.
[3] St. Mark ii. 27.   [4] Lev. and Num.

As years rolled on, and man, to evil prone,

Sought not his Maker's glory but his own,

The Highest chose one favoured tribe [1] among

Earth's many citizens (now but a throng

Of idol worshippers) and deigned to give

The precepts which, observing, they should live ; [2]

With trembling hearts affrighted Israel saw

The terrors heralding the moral law,

When from the mountain's burning crest they heard

The awful voice of the Eternal Word.

His Law proclaimed, He taught the statutes they

Should keep, believe, and reverence and obey,—

All types in which unclouded faith could see

Foreshadowings of a bright futurity.

In holy jealousy [3] the Lord ordained

His worthy worship. By His Word explained

---

[1] Gen. xvii.   [2] Exod. xx.

[3] Ezek. xxxix. 25.

The sacerdotal rites, the yearly Feasts,
The daily sacrifice, His chosen Priests;
The Sabbath rest; the year of Jubilee;
The great atonement made to cleanse and free
The nation from transgression's hidden stain,
And all the rites whereby they should retain
His favour, and from the exhaustless store
Of heavenly Love draw blessings evermore.[1]

Inspired by God, 'twas Israel's joy to frame
A dwelling worthy the All-Holy name—
Worthy! for all with willing hearts and hands
Vied in fulfilling the Divine commands;
Wise, heaven-taught men with skill and ardour wrought
Rare costly offerings, offered all unsought,
To deck the hallowed courts, perchance to leaven
The dross of earth with rainbow tints of heaven.
The outer court with hangings fenced around

---

[1] Lev., Num., Deut. xxviii. 1-15.

To screen from foot profane the hallowed ground;
The brazen altar on which daily dies
The morning and the evening sacrifice;
The brazen laver, symbol that from sin
All must be pure who'd dare to enter in.

Within—the Holy Place, one glorious blaze
Of varying, intermingling tints, displays
Its hangings, rich with many a gorgeous hue,
Bright scarlet, purple, and deep Tyrian blue;
Its walls with gold and silver overlaid,
Its holy altar gorgeously arrayed
In golden vesture. Every vessel told
Of wealth outpoured—a story writ in gold,—
A wealth which Egypt, terror-stricken, pressed
Profusely upon each departing guest.[1]
In fear[2] the smiter kissed the mightier rod,
And Egypt's spoils adorned the House of God.

[1] Exod. xii. 35, 36.   [2] Exod. xii. 33.

A thick embroidered vail droops and divides
The Holy and Most Holy Place, and hides
THE PRESENCE. For what eye can live and meet
The glory floating o'er the Mercy Seat;
And it, the ark, the cherubim all glow
With finest gold, man only can bestow
His best, his all, to honour the abode
Of an All-Holy, ever-present God.
And every part, its hues, proportions, all,
The priestly robes, the hangings, naught too small
For His creative hand, but all reflect
The wisdom of the Heavenly Architect.[1]

As Israel prospered and an earthly king
Ruled o'er their destinies, God deigned to fling
His wondrous wisdom as a mantle o'er
The suppliant monarch, and in holy love
Instructed well he reared a sacred shrine

[1] Exod. xxix.

More glorious for the Majesty Divine
Than the embroidered tent pitched by the band
Of shepherds, wandering to their promised land;
A nobler offering which might well express
The land's prosperity and thankfulness.[1]

The treasure stores of earth were opened wide,
Far distant lands their choicest wares supplied;
The temple rose, adorned with all the skill
Of earth's most noted artisans, until
The work in gorgeous splendour shone complete,
And clouds of glory o'er the mercy seat
Descending rolled, as God, accepting, blest
With heavenly fire His place of earthly rest.[2]

The Saviour died. The rage of envious man
Wrought in completing the predestined plan
Of man's salvation, all as was foretold
By seers and prophets in the days of old,

[1] 2 Chron. i.   [2] 1 Kings v., vi.; 2 Chron. ii.–vii.

Each scene prefigured all the law ordained,
Fulfilled in Him and man's redemption gained;
No more for sin a sinless victim dies—
Jesus has made a perfect sacrifice.[1]

Our God is Love.[2] We live beneath His sway;
His wisdom guides our footsteps day by day;
Each breath we breathe, each longing of the soul,
Each holy thought, which, bursting the control
Of sensuous earth, rejoices to be free,
Each hope of bliss throughout eternity,
Each act of love, the words of truth that fall
From man's frail lips, 'tis He inspires them all.[3]
Man hath no strength, but it from Jesus flows,
No love,[4] no life,[5] save that which He bestows;
Dumb, weak, and helpless, he might strive in vain
In his own strength to chaunt the feeblest strain,

---

[1] Heb. ix., x. 14.   [2] 1 Gen. Ep. St. John iv. 8.
[3] Acts xvii. 28 ; Ps. xxiii., xxviii. 7, 8.
[4] 1 Gen. Ep. St. John iv. 12.   [5] St. John xiv. 6.

But, taught of God, e'en he may hope to raise
On earth the echoes of angelic praise.

Wherewith shall man assay to rear a fame
Worthy the Holy God? It were in vain
To rend the Earth, its cavern depths explore
To grasp its priceless gems, its glittering ore;
The fairest spot that greets a mortal's eyes,
The rarest treasures bounteous earth supplies,
The artist's noblest skill, must even fall,
Unworthy Him, whose word created all;[1]
The costliest gift for grace may vainly sue,
The lowly mite may find acceptance due.[2]

To Him who taught the Israelites to raise
A noble temple in those ancient days,
And who is, too, our Lawgiver and King,
It well befits that we should freely bring
From 'midst the store of blessings He has blessed

[1] Acts vii. 48-50.   [2] St. Luke xxi. 4.

Whate'er we value most, the choicest, best,
And with no stinted, half-grudged tithes to twine
The decorations of His sacred shrine,
And tho' no human offering e'er can be
Worthy th' acceptance of the Deity
The earnest, thankful heart, with love imbued,
Yearns to outpour its fervent gratitude.

Shall we, whom God delights each day to bless
With some new theme for joy and thankfulness,
Shall this our land which bears from every shore
Its treasured spoils, an ever-growing store,
Exceeding far the proudest realms of old
In wealth of mortal and immortal gold,—
Shall each one haste to make his dwelling fair,
And leave God's temple naked, cold and bare?
Shall hall and palace with each other vie,
And castles rear their battlements on high,
And shall no beauty glisten in the shrine
Where God is worshipped? Shall His love divine

Awake no echoes? Shall His house express
Neglected, but a cold forgetfulness ? [1]

Let all unite to stud the wide world o'er
With temples worthy of the days of yore.
Let human skill in noblest efforts vie,
And fancy soar in wildest flights on high.
Let minds imbued with heavenly wisdom still
To God, the Giver,[2] consecrate their skill.
Nor shall the soul, inspired, create in vain,
Skilled hands shall work with willing hearts again ;
Embroidered hangings, bright with many a dye,
Which all the tints of ancient days outvie,
Rich painted windows, whose deep mellow tone
Is rivalled by the hand of Time alone,
The costliest metals, marbles rich and rare,
The granite rock, each stone, each beam shall bear
The glowing impress of a living art,
And speak the language of an ardent heart.

[1] 1 Chron. xvii.   [2] Acts xvii. 24, 25.

Let symbols still, as in the days of old,
The wonders of creative love unfold.
The eye shall lead the memory to recall
The mighty God whose word created all,—
His wondrous attributes of love and power,
His ever-present care, man's glorious dower,
The vast infinitudes which e'er fulfil
His wise decrees, the doers of His will,
The gracious sacrifice which love Divine
Alone could offer at the sacred shrine,
Which reared upon the rock that sin had riven
A ladder reaching to the gate of heaven.[1]
The Spirit, too, from sculptured stone shall cry,
And breathe again the strains of prophecy,
By works which He in wisdom has inspired
Shall distant generations' souls be fired,
The graven word for evermore proclaim
In emblematic guise God's endless fame.

[1] Gen. xxviii. 12.

Though earthly wealth and human skill combine

In noblest efforts to adorn His shrine,

And while thus fair the temple where we meet

To sue for mercy at the mercy-seat,

However glorious these, not these alone;

(This costly setting with no precious stone,

This is not worship;) unto Him must rise

The heart in suppliant and adoring sacrifice:

In vain the graceful spire up-points on high

If it directs no wanderer where to fly;

In vain the altar's beauty if unblest

With earnest worshippers, with love and zest;

In vain the daily ritual echoed there

If but the lips repeat the well-known prayer;

In vain the posture, vain the sacrifice,

Which nought save only custom sanctifies.[1]

Away with all that narrow-minded zeal

Which scorns a fervour 'tis not its to feel,

---

[1] Isa. i. 11-17; Ps. l. 7-14.

Which sees in hallowed forms but the display
Of soulless myths, or superstition's sway;
Which deems mere outward show all rites divine,
And digs but dross in worship's golden mine;
Which cavils even at the priestly dress,
Not that it lacketh faith or righteousness,[1]
But outer vestures, colours, black or white,—
O'er trifles such as these God's champions fight,
And deem it sin in costly robe to stand
Before His altar, whose divine command
Ordained the garments of His priests of old
Of varying colours, decked with gems and gold.[2]
Nor ceremonies, forms, and dress alone;
An altar's lawless if it be of stone;[3]
Its covering must be unembroidered, white,
No daylit candle shed an useless light,
And e'en the cross, which man would raise on high
As witness of his Saviour's victory,

---

[1] Exod. xxviii. ; Isa. xi. 5, lix. 17 ; Ps. cxxxii. 9, 16.
[2] Exod. xxviii.   [3] Bennett judgment.

As once the altar stood in Gilead's coasts

In token that they served the Lord of Hosts,[1]

This, too, awakes a superstitious dread

Lest it be worshipped in the Saviour's stead.

O draw the curtain o'er each vain pretence,

And mark the teachings of Omnipotence,

Ne'er stir up strife where all disputes should cease,

Nor strike wild discords on the harp of peace.

Why to the Eastward turn expectant eyes?

Why do we stand when strains of praise arise?

Why bow at Jesus' name? Why kneel to pray?

Why vest our priests in one prescribed array?

What are all forms? Vain, cold, and valueless;

An empty casket save when they express

The warm o'erflowings of a heart imbued

With love and awe, with faith and gratitude :

By these made holy, outward forms may be

A worthy offering to the Deity.[2]

[1] Josh. xxii.
[2] Mosaic Law—Exodus, Leviticus, Deuteronomy.

Let God be worshipped, let His praise be sung

With heart and voice; let children's joyous tongue

Swell the glad strains, until their echoes rise

Up to the Holy One, meet sacrifice.[1]

No paid performance of accustomed song,

No melody poured forth to lure the throng,

Who else perchance might scarce have entered there —

The stately music, one long bidding prayer—

But one full chorus, as from every soul

The joyous strains of adoration roll,

Heartfelt devotion, free from earthly leaven,

And meet to mingle with the praise of heaven.

Thus in one brotherhood,[2] with one accord

Let all unite to magnify the Lord;

Let worthy offerings beautify His shrine,

And humble worship glow with life divine,

So shall the Highest from His throne above

---

[1] Ps. cxlviii.–cl.   [2] Heb. iii. 1.

Accept the sacrifice of faith and love.

As o'er the mercy-seat in days of old

The glory of the Lord in fulness rolled,

So all unseen His glorious presence still

As in the days of old His courts shall fill;

Bid earthly longing, earthly tumult cease,

And o'er His people shed His heavenly Peace.[1]

1861.

---

[1] S. Luke xxiv. 36.

A DREAM

Chill blows the breath of the evening
    After the heat of the day.
Toil on its vaunting wings,
Severs its leading strings,
Old aspirations flings
    Far away.

Wild howls the gathering tempest,
    Storm clouds are hovering nigh.
Circled in molten light,
High on Truth's topmost height,
Sits Justice, throned on right.
    Shall Justice die?

Solemn the notes of her requiem
　　Float o'er the graves of the dead.
Light of the ruddy morn,
Rose of the tangled thorn,
Oath of the falsely sworn,
　　Blood idly shed.

Tremble, O star of ill-omen !
　　Hide 'neath the lightning's blue glare.
Law of the years to be,
Chains of the seeming free,
Crown of true honesty,
　　Falsehood stripped bare.

Butler & Tanner, The Selwood Printing Works. Frome, and London.